"He kne[illegible]
and ha[illegible]
time... [illegible]
dominoes."

Cullen Gallagher, *Pulp Serenade*

"Tight plotting, masterful pacing, characters whose desperation you can feel. Harry Whittington delivers every time."

Bill Crider, author of the
Sheriff Dan Rhodes series

"Whittington does the best sheer story-telling since the greatest days of the detective pulps."

Anthony Boucher, *New York Times*

"Harry Whittington was the king of plot and pace."

Joe R. Lansdale, author of the
Hap and Leonard series

"Harry Whittington was one of the half-dozen most consistently inventive and entertaining of all the writers who specialized in paperback originals during the 1950s and 1960s."—

Bill Pronzini, author of the
"Nameless" Detective series

A HAVEN FOR THE DAMNED

by Harry Whittington

Introduction by David Laurence Wilson

Black Gat Books • Eureka California

A HAVEN FOR THE DAMNED

Published by Stark House Press
1315 H Street
Eureka, CA 95501
griffinskye3@sbcglobal.net
www.starkhousepress.com

ISBN: 1-933586-75-3
ISBN-13: 978-1-933586-75-5

Book design by Mark Shepard, shepgraphics.com

First Stark House Press Edition: May 2015

A Convocation of Ghosts
By David Laurence Wilson

It's a bittersweet feeling, sometimes, to see a new edition of a favored novel.

To celebrate a new edition of *A Haven For The Damned,* I could think of nothing more pleasing than to reacquaint myself with the 1962 original, when Harry Whittington (1915-1989), was still trying to slay dragons, both his own and those of his society. Until now, that slim volume, 144 pages, has been the only route to this *Haven.*

One of the first things you'll notice is the price: thirty-five cents, the like of which you are unlikely to see again. The cover is not exceptional, though after 52 years, it's done a good job of holding the book together. It's a little beaten up — a little dirty and aged — but the pages are intact. No one ever put on gloves to read a Whittington yarn — so the book looks just as it should. Veterans should get a little dispensation for creaky spines.

On the cover a man and woman are standing in what looks like moonlight. He's in Levis and boots. She's wearing what might be a party dress and high heels. He has his hands around her head, caressing her, his lips against hers, and both of their faces are obscured by the angle of the embrace and kiss. The woman is willing but her posture is out of place, tentative, her hands on her hips, those high heels planted shoulder width. She is centered, like a wrestler, and one way or another, she is definitely going to smack this amorous cowboy.

You might say this is just one artist's interpretation, like the swelling breasts on the cover of a W. Somerset Maugham paper-back. It would have fit onto the cover of almost any of Harry's novels.

On the back of this volume are, in a sense, the directions: "A town by the name of Lust," a strip of weathered, abandoned buildings that has itself been damned.

Harry Whittington had a long association with lust, its pros and cons, and though he didn't often use the word, the publishers couldn't seem to avoid it—no fewer than six of his novels featured the "lust" in their titles, everything from *Lust Farm* to *Mask of Lust*. It came off as a brand name.

But don't get the wrong idea. This was not just a quick roll in the hay but a long sustained effort that preoccupied not just Harry's career but his life. As the medium ebbed and flowed, so did Harry. He was not limited to any one publisher, any one category; Harry and his publishers used nearly 20 different pseudonyms to announce the writers of his novels: westerns, crime novels, stories of the rural south, nurse, Hollywood, war and spy novels, novelizations and stories "based" on *The Man From U.N.C.L.E.*

There is really no single work that serves best to introduce Harry Whittington, no bestseller or big movie title. To really explain Harry you'd have to carry around a substantial bookcase. You could only fit a taste of his work, just a sample, into a suitcase or bag.

Many of the people and events in Harry's life have already been described, most notably in three earlier collections from Stark House.

Along with his financial needs, one reason Harry wrote so many stories is that he just couldn't leave his stories alone. He was so good at generating "what-ifs," variations on his settings, plots and characters, that the roads not taken could become a whole series of novels. Readers familiar with Harry's novels will find echoes of *A Moment To Prey, Desert Stake-Out*, and others along the road leading to *A Haven For The Damned*.

If we return to Harry's town with the aid of a dictionary, we're reminded that "lust" is actually a "desire" or "intense enthusiasm," just as "suspense" is a "state of usually anxious uncertainty." Both "lust" and "suspense" are about wanting something, not necessarily about getting it. It's a landscape filled with people who are not parallel, not intersecting, but skewed.

A Whittington story is when the "lust" and "suspense" come together in a middle or working-class neighborhood. It's the larcenous brother, the wandering mate, the murder scene across the street, and the bloody hand that pulls you from a warm bed. Harry's novels are survival manuals, a series of tips on how to get back to normalcy. Sometimes they work.

To your advantage, this is a lesser-known Whittington, one of the stories he wrote when his own world was being challenged as thoroughly as the lives of his characters. By the time of the late 'fifties, Harry was in competition with the books he had already written. *A Haven For The Damned* was one of the books that was hard to sell. Treasure it; it could have easily become a pile of ashes.

A Haven For the Damned was sold to Fawcett Publications in 1960 but was not published until 1962. This was a big part of the problem. Paperbacks themselves were in recession.

In his own bibliography, the record of his sales, Harry divided his career — and really, his life, since there was so little separation — into "The Unpublished Years," "Published — The Beginning Years," "The Cadillac Years" (a good, 12-year run, and yes, this is when Harry did purchase a Cadillac — and drove it home to the consternation of his wife, who said, "But we're not Cadillac people...") and then "The Lean and Savage Years." This is when the market wanted sex from him and he provided it, under a series of concealing disguises. In the volumes promising "Flesh," "Hell," "Sin" "Shame" and "Passion" you can still find Harry, if you know where to look, though to Harry's relief, this recognition was only identified in retrospect. When the going became tough, *A Haven For The Damned* is one of the templates that shows us what Whittington wanted to be writing.

After this period, in 1968, Harry dropped out for six years. He returned to full-time writing in 1974 but now the results were historical novels, books subject to bloating. Despite the excess pages and historical dressing, you could still find Harry in the stories from "Ashley Carter" and "Blaine Stevens." Harry ended his career with this late success, an unexpected third act.

A *Haven For The Damned* is a novel that offers many pleasures. It's a modern western with no horses, no Indians, a territory visited infrequently. Harry was very good at this kind of story. In this one his characters deal with death and desperation in a town like the set of a Samuel Beckett play. They are isolated and disoriented, none of them completely whole or satisfied. It comes from a moment in his personal history when Harry must have felt the same. He must have wondered if he was all along writing a script for himself.

This introduction is for the fan, not to persuade someone to read it but to set the scene, to persuade the reader to approach it with the proper reverence. Whittington was and still is, "The King of the Paperbacks."

What better way to end this introduction than with a quote from Harry, a good, long quote. Just start on page one ... you'll thank me.

—Dana Point, California
December, 2014

A HAVEN FOR THE DAMNED

by Harry Whittington

I

On an almost inaccessible escarpment, 3500 feet above sea level, on Burro mountain in the Variadero ranges, somewhere between Lordsburg and Socorro, sprawls an abandoned settlement once known as Lust, New Mexico. Its half-dozen buildings, aslant with dry-rot, slowly decay in the desert sun. Three-quarters of a century ago it was a thriving town alive with cries of silver miners and prospectors, but for a long time now it has been dead, dying of malnutrition, poverty and creeping paralysis: fifteen years ago, frantic men with Geiger counters once more abandoned it to lizards and horned toads and the lonely cry of owls.

One day last fall, seven people arrived separately in Lust, New Mexico, and found one man already there.

They came, oddly, on several different roads that all somehow led to this lost place, almost by design, like various colored threads wound together on the same skein.

These people reached a dreadful moment of crisis in Lust, New Mexico; time had run out for each of them, and only time could give them a second chance at life.

But the really strange aspect wasn't that they did come to Lust, New Mexico, but that they found it at all, considering its isolation, the way it had sagged recumbent and forgotten for so long, and how difficult it was to find, even when you looked for it on purpose. New Mexico maps ceased marking, or listing it, thirty-five years ago.

The green Chevy sedan had been squatting in the first parking place outside the Yucca City National Bank since seven o'clock that Tuesday morning in October. At precisely 8 A.M. somebody punched a coin into the curb meter, buying two hours of parking time, which was the legal time-limit for parking on Main Street during business hours.

It was a hot, sweaty morning. Nobody paid any attention to the green Chevy, because traveling men often parked at this curb when they spent the night at the Yucca Hotel across the street.

By 9 A.M. the white heat of the sun was like blazing rays through a cosmic magnifying glass, and a small crowd was hugging the double glass doors, impatient to be the first ones inside the air-conditioned bank.

But when the doors were unlocked by the bank guard, they were thrust outward violently, and the knot of people staggered back, gaping.

Three men burst through the doorway and ran toward the green Chevy sedan.

In the lead, a tall, broad-shouldered man in a light blue suit, black Oxfords, gray felt hat and stocking mask carried a gun in one hand and a black suitcase in the other. The bag was so heavy that he listed slightly under its weight, big as he was.

The man in the middle wasn't armed at all. In shirtsleeves and slacks, sandy hair wild and eyes wide, he was young and brawny and broad, but he was helpless because the third man held a gun jammed against his spine, and had a fist twisted in his belt.

This last man was of medium height, in a dark suit, dark shoes, felt hat and stocking mask covering his face.

He was propelling the helpless young man in a way that kept him stumbling just off-balance, and was crouching behind him, as if using the larger body for a shield.

The people gasped, and some of them said, "That's Matt Bishop they got there with them."

"That's Matt Bishop, all right."

"Look. They got Matt Bishop."

But Matt just looked at them, his ordinarily heavy-lidded, drowsy eyes empty of anything. He appeared stunned, crabbed along the walk toward the green sedan by the stocky man with a hand twisted in Matt's belt.

The man in front, reaching the car, whirled and spoke over his shoulder, just one sharp word: "Burn."

"Just go, man. Don't worry about me," called the masked man behind Matt.

Nobody in the crowd moved, but the bank guard worked his gun from its holster and ran through the glass doors to the walk. He halted, squinting across the sun, gun held out at arms' length in front of him

"Hey!" the bank guard shouted.

The stocky man hurled a quick gander across his shoulder and swore. But before the bank guard could fire, he lunged forward, jerking Matt Bishop around, between him and the guard.

The guard was already pressing the trigger and was unable to stop, even when he saw to his horror that he was going to shoot Matt Bishop and there wasn't any way on earth to avoid it.

The gun roared, and the sound rattled in the quiet morning street, reverberating off the buildings across it, their show windows quivering.

The bullet struck Matt Bishop low in the left side. It connected with such impact that it hurled both Matt and the masked man four feet along the curb. Matt struck against the front fender of the green sedan before they stopped moving.

Matt sagged and would have crumpled to the walk, but the stocky man clutched him with both hands around the middle, as he might hoist a sack of grain and staggered backward with him half the length of the car.

The tall man had thrown open the rear door of the sedan, tossing the suitcase in on the floor. He wheeled around and both of them caught at Matt Bishop to pour him through the door.

Matt was no longer aware where he was.

He was suddenly cold all over and his teeth were chattering with cold. He heard them cursing him because his legs were dragging on the walk, but he could not help it. His legs were dead weight, as if he were paralysed, and his legs felt as cold as ice.

There was this flat taste of blood in his mouth. He thought, in a strangely detached way: his own blood. He had been shot by the bank guard. He had never thought Greenie could hit the side of a barn, but it looked like he was wrong. Wrong again? He was wrong again, and he was dying. Oh, fine. What a lovely time to die. "Goodbye, Susie. Forgive me, Susie."

"Goodbye, Susie. Forgive me, Susie." Where'd he heard those words before? His national anthem? His endless refrain. It was what he said to Susie now instead of "I love you."

Well, it didn't matter any more.

The two men thrust Matt into the rear of the sedan and he sprawled across the back seat. His arm toppled over against the suitcase on the floor beside him.

He stared at that black suitcase crammed with money, and he could not care less.

He heard the car start. "Fifteen minutes from now they'll find this green Chevy abandoned outside town, and won't know what hit 'em. These hicksvilles," the big man said. He was at the wheel.

Matt felt the car burn away from the curb into the mild flow of traffic.

His head whirled dizzily and he whispered, frantic, "Doctor.... You got to get me to a doctor."

The stocky man half-turned on the front seat and stared at Matt. He was laughing. "Listen to that," he said. "He must be making like jokes."

"Yeah. That's him, all right," the tall man said through his nylon mask. He did not take his eyes off the street. "He keeps you laughing like that all the time."

2

At ten o'clock Wednesday night, Susie Bishop snapped off the lights in her living room.

She walked through the dark hall, turned on a light in her bedroom and then hurried back along the hallway to the living room. She stood at a window with the house in darkness, except for the bedroom light.

She pinched aside the curtains and stared into the street. They were out there.

There were two cars, each parked half a block from her house and facing each other in the night.

"What are you going to do, Susie?" Her mother moved out of the darkness toward her.

"Mother. I told you. Please go back to the bedroom."

"What are you going to do?"

Susie released the curtain, turned, exasperated. "Mother — I'm going to do — just what you know damned well I've got to do."

"No, Susan. I don't know anything of the kind — "

"Then go back to the bedroom, Mother, and stay there the way you promised!" Susie spoke in a rapid, breathless way, tension making her words spill faster than ever — she always spoke in an almost musical chant. "You promised. You said you wouldn't interfere."

"I only promised to give you time to come to your senses. You've had all day now — and — "

"Oh, my God, yes. I've had all day. The longest day in my life. The very longest." Her hand tightened on the map she'd carried since she found it pushed under the door when she went out to get the morning newspaper.

She didn't know how it had been accomplished, but some time last night somebody had crept silently to her front porch and slipped this map, inside an envelope, under her door.

Her fists tightened. She had not mentioned what else she found with the map; she tried not even to think about the blood-soaked handkerchief. It was Matt's handkerchief, Matt's blood. She knew this instinctively; she'd have known it was Matt's handkerchief even without the monogram "MB" in the corner. A handkerchief she'd given him. And the blood. It was like a message, a threat, a warning from those killers.

She had hidden the bloody handkerchief in her pocketbook and not even mentioned it to her mother. The map was enough — a circle drawn on it and the crudely printed words: "Alone. Now."

Hands shaking she had closed the front door, staring at map and handkerchief.

She recognized the area marked on that map, and a shock went through her, an unexplained sense of wrong.

The place marked on that map was an inaccessible mountain where she and Matt had gone once on a hunting trip. Matt had wanted to hunt and she'd been pleased to be alone with him. He said Burro Mountain, and that whole range, was a place where a man might lose himself. Whole mountain ranges and mesas and deep canyons were lost inside greater ranges.

She felt ill, thinking how strange it was that these men should choose Burro Mountain for a hiding place. Almost as if Matt might have suggested it, knowing she could find it.

She shook her head, admitting this didn't make sense. Matt had been shot, might be near death. If those men chose that place, it was only because it was hidden, incredibly huge and lonely.

She went on talking now, to her mother, remembering the way she felt finding that map, that blood-stained handkerchief.

"Five A.M. I found this map at five o'clock this morning. I went out to get the paper, and I was never so glad to see the daylight. I lay in that bed last night and I prayed for the darkness to end, and it was never going to end, and then it did end, and there was daylight, but now I had found this map, and it all started for me all over again.... Only now I was praying for night to come."

"You must go to the police with this. You've simply got to, Susan. I've a splitting headache thinking about it. I've had a splitting headache all day, and that's the only answer. You've got to go to the police." Susan's mother was in her early forties. She weighed a hundred and twenty pounds, underweight for her age and height, but men still found her attractive, and this pleased her because she looked so trim and youthful at forty. There was this same chanting quality in Susan's mother's voice, but not the music that gave Susan's breathless way of speaking all its charm.

"Well! I don't have to go to them. Oh, no. They've come to me. Since six o'clock this morning knocking on that front door. And they're still out there —" Susan jerked back the shade, nodding toward the moon-tipped street. "See them? See those stupes? I don't know, I simply don't know if they are out there guarding me, or are they watching the house to see if Matt will come here with the loot?"

"Susan, how can you say such a thing? Everybody feels terrible about what happened to Matt."

She shrugged, staring through the window. "Well, look at them down there in those two cars. Oh, they're so subtle. So damned subtle. As if any crook on earth couldn't smell them six blocks away. I'm not even a crook and they don't fool me. Parked in the dark street with their headlights off and their beady little eyes watching this house —"

"Susan, they're out there to protect you. If you had an ounce of reason left, you'd understand that."

Susie dropped the curtain and paced the darkened room, stepping around Matt's bowling bag and bowling shoes where they had been put out, waiting for him to come home last night.

She prowled in the darkness, not bumping anything because she knew this house as she knew her own heart, and where her nose was, and where her breasts were when Matt reached for her in their bed in the night. She knew where her heart was then, and how it pounded for him, pounded like crazy, even after four years, even after people began giving her odd, doubting smiles when she talked about Matt and how much she loved him.

She was a slender girl, with rich black hair and a long curved throat and deep violet eyes.

She swung her arm suddenly, speaking in a singing, protesting way. "All right, Mother. Maybe I'd understand a lot of things if I had any reason left. But why should I have any reason left? They've hounded me. All day long. Have I heard from my husband? Have I had any word? You'll get in touch with us, Mrs. Bishop, if you hear from Matt, won't you? And all I know is that Matt was shot, and is maybe dying, and maybe dead. I don't even know if he's dead, and always I thought I would know the instant he were dead, because if he were dead then I would be dead, too, inside. But now I'm just numb. Too numb to think, too numb to live, or care about anything.... All I know is — all I know on earth is that Matt wants me to come to him, and I'm going!"

"You don't know that, Susan! You don't know anything of the kind. All you know is that this morning you found that dirty map of New Mexico inside a filthy envelope under your front door, and that the map has a circle around a ghost town in the Variadero ranges — a town not even named on the map. That's all you know."

"I know that's where Matt may be. Maybe they've got him there, and maybe he's still alive, and if he's alive, I've got to help him. If I'd known you were going to start in on me at this hour, I'd have run you out of here this morning — "

"Susan. Such a terrible way to talk. To your own mother."

"My God, you're not much of a mother if you pay any attention to anything I say right now ... I'm crazy, Mother. Right now, I'm half crazy ... I love you — but even you must know this is the only chance I've got, and I've got to take it."

"Why are you going to that place — alone?"

"Because that's the only place I know to go. That's all I know to do. Isn't that a good enough reason?"

"No. You've got to go to the police. They'll send somebody with you —"

"And those people — whoever they are that took Matt with them, they'll see the police with me, and they'll kill Matt if he's still alive. They'd kill him before we could get near them ... and you know it."

"I don't know it. I don't know anything about the police, either, but I do know they'd know what to do about that map — why, there might even be fingerprints on that envelope."

"Mother!" Susan whispered, but her voice was so tense, so vibrant with the frantic anxieties inside her, that she gave the effect of screaming. "Please. Try to understand me. I don't want the police. I don't give a damn in hell for the police, or that bank, or their money, or if the bank gets their money back or not. I'm only thinking about Matt. Can't you understand that? I've got this marked map. It's all I've got. Matt may be up in those mountains. I've got to go there and find out. It's that simple."

"Suppose it was just some — some crank — some idiot playing a joke?"

"Oh... !" The words spilled now across Susan's lips like muted music of anguish, in the low registers, sustained, hurting. "Don't you think I thought of that, first thing? An idiot, playing an idiot's prank? That's more likely the answer than that I'll find Matt alive after I've driven these hundreds of miles tonight. But then I know I have no choice, either way. Isn't this whole damned thing an idiot's prank? Two escaped convicts robbing a bank that hasn't been robbed since — Billy the Kid! — and taking Matt along as hostage, and Matt getting shot, and maybe killed, and he's all I've got, and I love him, and we never hurt anybody, never hurt anybody on this earth, and yet Matt was shot — and not either one of those — those monsters! They weren't hurt, but Matt was shot. Isn't that an idiot's prank? Isn't it? So I have no choice. I've got to go to this place, and I must go alone ... and I want you to go back in that bedroom. When I've been gone out the back door for ten minutes, I want you to turn out that light, and don't answer the door, or the phone, or any soul on earth, until morning ... you've got to give me that much start, you've got to ... or I'll never forgive you, and I'll hate you forever.... The only reason I let you stay here at all today is because you promised."

She did not wait to hear her mother answer. She found a lightweight sweater that was lavender in the light but looked gray in this darkness. She found her small handbag and she grasped it in her fist with the map; she looked around the room one last time, but she did not go near her mother, or speak to her again.

"Susan — "

But Susan was moving through the hallway, going into the dining room and across it to the kitchen. "Susan — "

Her mother moved along the hallway, vaguely illumined in faint light from the rear bedroom. She moved woodenly, hand pressed against her mouth, and when she reached the dining room, she heard the whisper of sound as Susan went out the back door into the night. She leaned against the door jamb staring into the darkness, her hand pressed against her mouth.

Susan walked slowly across the backyard, keeping to the deepest shadows, going steadily without bumping anything, seeing as a cat sees in the dark. I can see in the dark the way a cat does, she thought exultantly. I can move quickly in the dark the way a cat does, because I've got to.

At the alley, she paused, pressed hard in the shadows. The police might be out there in the alley. She didn't think so. All day they'd watched from the front, patrolling the alley every half hour.

The alley was quiet and she remained, breathless, waiting until she couldn't endure the waiting any more. Then she ran down the alley.

She covered her mouth with her hand to blot the sound of her breathing.

She reached the street, crossed it, and went running down the next alley. She felt good now — she had it made, she was beyond the reach of the police, and she was going in free, the way she used to do when she was a tomboy and played games better than any of the boys she knew.

It was a long way to her mother's house, but she was still running when she crossed her yard. The backs of her legs trembled. It was a long time since she'd been a tomboy! She was out of breath, breathing like an old woman. Breathing the way Matt made her breathe sometimes when he drove her wild. Matt. Oh, Matt. But she had to stop thinking about Matt, because she was all right as long as she didn't think about Matt at all.

Her mother's gray Dodge was parked in the driveway, as her mother had promised she'd leave it. This was her only hope of escaping the police guard even for a few hours. Her own car was in her garage where the cops could watch it to their hearts' content. Her mother was asleep back in her house, and barring some terrible emergency, no policeman would approach that house before nine o'clock tomorrow morning.

She had over ten hours head start on anyone who might follow her.

She opened the car door, slid in under the wheel, fumbled in her purse for ignition keys.

She listened to the hum of the motor, and then reversed, going out of the drive. She straightened the wheels, heading west out of Yucca City before she snapped on her headlights.

She clung to the steering wheel, feeling the world fly past her on the wind in the night. Somehow she was sure the world she had always known, and felt so secure in, was being blown away on the night wind, and was never going to be the same for her again.

What did she hope to accomplish? She didn't know. All she could think was that Matt might be up there, and she had to go to him.

She laughed in an abrupt, bitter way, aware she was still clutching that map in her fist as she had been holding it all this eternal day. And the really funny part of it was, she didn't even need that map at all any more.

It was spread out like a clean clear picture in her brain.

3

At six o'clock Thursday morning, a young man driving a dusty Plymouth pulled off highway 85 into the parking area outside a combination motel-restaurant with a Texaco gas station out front.

The motel was an angular, smart-looking imitation of the old adobe Texas ranch-houses once found along cattle trails. A cottonwood with a nine foot trunk-spread shaded a milky-blue swimming pool.

The young man rolled the Plymouth to a gas pump and sat staring toward the motel, as if counting the cars parked outside its rooms.

The sun was already glinting in the dust coated on the car and its windows.

The station attendant spoke to him.

Reed jerked his head around, looking at the attendant without really seeing him. "What?"

"I said, you wanta rent a room or you want gas?"

The young man exhaled heavily. "Fill it up ... And would you wash off the windows?"

"Sure. No charge... You want a room?"

"No... I'll get a cup of coffee." He glanced at the restaurant. "I leave the keys, you can pull it out of the way when you're through. Okay?"

"Sure. No charge."

Reed got out of the Plymouth then, aching, stretching upward from the small of his back. He glanced once more toward the cars parked outside the motel rooms, checking them. He winced, closing his eyes tightly against the thin lances of the sun.

He breathed out heavily once more and crossed the asphalt drive to the gleaming chrome-and-glass diner.

Watching him, the attendant frowned mildly, then shook his head, puzzled. You saw all kinds. You sure did.

Reed opened the restaurant door and then stood there a moment, eyes haggard, red-rimmed and sleepless. He brushed the flat of his hand down along the wrinkled front of his checked Orlon jacket, smoothing at it without even knowing he did it.

He was a slender man in his late twenties, tall, and as firm in the leg muscles and belly muscles and chest muscles as he had been at eighteen.

But preoccupied as he was, he admitted he was wound too tight, like a cheap clock that stops running because it's overwound, with its spring ready to burst, flying apart. He knew this about himself. Oh fine. What did you do? What in hell could you do about it?

With early sunlight behind him and a fluorescent gray cast across him from inside the diner, he appeared cold, withdrawn, detached, but very tired. This was the lie, that look of detachment. His nerves were raw, exposed, and though he barely spoke above a hoarse whisper, he was ready to scream out with the rages inside him, ready to break everything in his world that was not already smashed.

He looked at the few people at the tables, checked the truck drivers and the salesman at the counter. He frowned. There were couples in the booths. He walked the length of the room, looking at the people in the booths. Then he returned to the counter.

The waitress stood there waiting for him, a glass of iced water in her hand. She was a tired blonde woman in her thirties. She looked as if she had been dieting. She was laughing at him, in a private-joke manner that she didn't care to share.

"You satisfied?" she said to him.

"What?"

She laughed again. "You seen everything you want to see?"

He looked at her across the counter; for the moment anguish flashed deep in his green eyes, and for that second there was a wild, uncontrollable rage jerking at the muscles just under the surface of his face.

But when he spoke, his voice was low. "I'd like a cup of coffee, if you please." It was as if it required greater efforts all the time to control himself.

"Are you all right, mister?" She was frowning, troubled. She'd seen the rage, the flash of lightning deep in the green of his tired eyes. She couldn't forget it.

He stared at her, blandly. "You must have your own woes, sister. Could I have a cup of coffee, please?"

"Sure... anything else?"

He breathed in deeply. "No. That's all."

She moved away, frowning. She ran his coffee from a three-gallon chrome container. She was watching him from the corner of her eye. The coffee spilled over, scalding her thumb.

She cursed and one of the truck drivers laughed. "Trouble, Marge?" he said to her.

"Nothing I can't handle, Sandy." She brought Reed's coffee, sucking at her scalded thumb.

She set the cup before him, waiting for him to mention her thumb. He did not lift his head, or speak to her. He sat watching steam rise from the black coffee; it was unspeakably hot against his dry eyes.

The waitress walked away and stood talking in undertones to the man behind the cash register. He was a slender man, balding, in his forties, with a thin, long, sun-leathered face, a scrawny neck, spotless white shirt and streaked apron.

They glanced at Reed, whispering. The man left the cash register, came along the counter. He stopped near Reed, removed the plastic hood from the pastry plate and began rearranging the buns.

"Morning," he said.

Reed glanced up, but seemed to be looking through him.

"Traveled a long way last night, eh?"

"I guess so."

"You guess so?" the counter man laughed. "This here is Nara Pueblo, New Mexico, mister."

"Is it?"

"Sure is. Nara Pueblo. Mex talk. Means orange pueblo. Whatever pueblo means, huh?"

"Sounds fine."

"How far you say you come last night?"

"Why?" Reed looked up.

"Oh, now, wait a copper-pecking minute, mister. I'm just being friendly. Don't get me wrong. I'm one of the good ones. You know? Like the fellow says. It's just — well, you look bushed.

You know? Like you been driving all night. Or — drinking all night. Huh?"

"Does it make any difference?"

The smile faded. "No... Hell, I mean whether you was drinking? Or driving? Why, hell no. Not to me."

Reed looked up, abruptly, as if seeing the man for the first time. He stared at him, intently, so the counterman craned his neck, sucked air through his teeth, touched at his shirt collar self-consciously.

Reed spoke in a soft, yet compulsive tone, gentle, with violence crackling under it. "I been driving, mister. All night... All day yesterday, I think — "

"You think?"

"I think so. You said the name of this place — "

"Yeah. Sure. Nara Pueblo."

"No. No. No, not the town. What state?"

"What state? My God, mister, you kidding?"

"No. I'm not kidding. You said the name of the state. It don't matter, but you said it. What state?"

"New Mexico." He shook his head. "Mister, you better go back there in that motel, get you a room, and sleep it off."

"No. I'm all right. I haven't got — time. I didn't know what state it was. But — driving — you get like that. Driving a long time. Like, maybe you see a sign, or somebody tells you you're in New Mexico, but it doesn't matter except that you're finally out of Texas, and you're thankful for that — "

"That's pretty good. You're finally out of Texas, and you're thankful for that. That's pretty good."

"What?" Reed said absently.

"You just need about ten hours of good sleep, mister. You just need to rest."

The waitress had returned while they were talking and was leaning against the counter beside the counterman, watching Reed.

Reed shook his head. "No. I can't rest. I tried that. Yesterday... I think it was yesterday. I went into a motel and laid down... and tried to sleep. But I can't sleep... I might as well keep driving."

"You'll kill somebody, mister — "

"What?" Reed's head jerked up.

"Why, I just said, you'll kill somebody, driving as tired as you are. Or — you'll kill yourself."

"I can't sleep. I'm looking for somebody."

"What?" The counterman stared at him.

Reed looked up. He didn't want to talk about it. He didn't want to say anything about her. What did they care? It was nobody's affair but his own, and he knew better than to go around yakking about it. But lately it hadn't seemed to matter what he wanted to do, or knew he should do. Lately he couldn't help himself. He thought about her all the time, and he found himself blurting it out, talking about her, even to strangers. Like now.

"I'm looking for my wife," Reed said.

The waitress burst into sudden mocking laughter, covering her mouth with her hand. Her third finger was taped with a Band-aid.

Reed scowled, turning his head slowly and looking at the waitress.

"You're — looking for your wife?" the counterman said.

The waitress giggled again, not looking at Reed. "I could of told you," she said. "I knew it. When he walked in. I knew. I been up and down a lot of roads and I seen it — "

"Shut up, Margie," the counterman said. He swallowed, his Adam's apple working against the leathery strings of his flesh. "Mister, it ain't going to do you no good to keep looking, beat as you are."

Reed nodded, tried to concentrate on his coffee. He chewed at his mouth. He looked up suddenly.

"Maybe you saw her?" His voice was hoarse with urgency in it.

The counterman shrugged. "Might. If she come in here. But a lot of people come in here — "

"No." Reed shook his head. "No. Not a lot of people like her. If — she came in here, you'd know her. She's a blonde." Reed stared at the waitress. "A real blonde." The waitress made a sniffing noise of disdain, but Reed was no longer aware of her. "A real blonde, and her hair is wild because she wears it in a French roll... you know she's lazy, it comes loose around her face. And her face is — is full, like a little girl's face, but — she's not a little girl. She has pale blue eyes, and pale skin, and her lips are bright red, bright red. She's got — got an awfully good body — and — if you saw her — she was with a man, about fifty, big fellow, broad, in tailored suit, smokes — smokes expensive cigars. If — "

He stopped talking. He saw the waitress glance at the counter-man. The waitress grinned, turning her face away.

"They were in here," Reed said. "Weren't they?"

"Hell, I don't know."

"When? When were they in here? How long ago?"

"Oh, now, hell, mister, I don't know. I don't know about that. There was this blonde girl. And this elderly man. That was — yesterday — they were talking about this short-cut, trying to make up some time they had lost — and I tried to warn them. You got to know the roads if you get off the main highways in this state, but they didn't even listen to me.... Now, wait, I got no idea it was the same folks at all ...."

4

That same Thursday morning, about nine o'clock, on highway 85, Sheriff Ben Pritchard was on his way to his office in the county seat. A pink blur raced past him like a jet, and his car trembled in the backwash. Angered, Ben whipped the car around in the middle of the highway and tromped the accelerator, going in pursuit.

It was a long chase in the hot morning. His tires sang with the heat and the friction in them. But Ben Pritchard was mule-headed and single-minded and had inherited a very wide streak of German-brand stubbornness from his maternal grandmother.

The green-and-white sheriff's car drew alongside the speeding pink Cadillac, its red signal whirling and siren wailing.

The sheriff took his hand off the steering wheel just long enough to wave imperiously toward the curbing. Both cars slowed; still, it required a good five hundred yards of highway to bring the two cars to rest on the slate-and alkali-crusted shoulders.

For a moment Ben sat, gripping the steering wheel before he

got out of his car.

He walked slowly. His hands were still shaking and his ruddy face was bloodless. He was a tall, lean man in his middle thirties with sun-seasoned flesh and bleached blue eyes.

He pushed his flat-crowned trooper's hat back on his dark hair, and bending over, stared at the two people in the Cadillac.

"What the hell is this?" he said, and his voice was shaking, too. "I'm the goddamn sheriff of this goddamn county and it ain't my job to haul in speedsters, but this is ridiculous. You got any idea how fast you were going, mister?"

The man in the Cadillac licked his lips. "Sheriff, I'm sorry. Maybe I was in a bit of a hurry — "

"A bit of a hurry? Jesus H. Christ — "

"Sheriff, my name is Harvey Duncan. Harvey J. Duncan and — " Then the big man stopped talking, thinking what difference did it make? Harvey J. Duncan. What did that name matter out here? What did it really matter anywhere, he wondered, except to him? It mattered to him. And he had spent fifty-two years trying to make it matter to other people.

He winced. All this running, and here he was stopped by a hick sheriff in some desolate county, who had never heard of him, and wouldn't care if he had.

"Tell him, Harve," the girl said, nudging the man.

Sheriff Pritchard stopped shaking slightly now and bent a little more at the waist, staring past the man at the girl on the other side of the seat.

She twisted a little under his scrutiny, wrinkling her eyes in a faint, halting smile when she saw him looking at her body. She didn't mind his looking at her body. She appeared pleased. She had a really dazzling body all right, and it seemed she loved it almost as much as did every man who saw it.

"Never mind, Milly," Duncan said. His brown hair was still thick, and he wore it parted on the side and brushed back; it stayed neatly in place, dry. The sheriff envied a man who could brush his hair in place without hair oil.

He frowned. "Tell me what?" He watched them. This Duncan was at least thirty years older than the chick. At least thirty. "Tell me what?"

"Nothing, officer. It's all right." Duncan said. He was a man who never apologized for anything he did, and now he was not offering apology, he was merely in a hurry and attempting diplomacy with a public servant. "Sorry about the speed. I'm sorry I was exceeding your speed limit. I'll try to hold it down."

"Well, no... I'm afraid that won't be good enough." Ben frowned. "I'll have to take you folks in — "

"Take us where?" the girl said. She turned on the seat, facing Ben, her dress twisting higher up on her thigh. She glanced in a troubled way through the rear window, chewing on a full under-lip.

"Where must you take us?" Duncan stirred in a slightly nervous way inside his two-hundred dollar, all-season suit. The kind that never showed wrinkles, the sheriff thought, touched with envy, never showed wrinkles, not even if you wallowed around in it all day. And if this character did anything except wallow around all day with that blonde chick beside him, the whole world had gone nuts, all right.

"Into the county seat," he said. "I'll have to take you folks into the county seat." He pulled his gaze back from the pink thighs and the tailored suit. Funny, the inside of this car smelled rich, with the smell of mink (after the furriers had cleaned it up, of course) and the smell of expensive perfume and expensive cigars, and expensive luggage in the back seat. The careless rich smell, everything tossed around, and good smelling. The whole deal smelled rich, and there was, too, the smell of wrong about it all.

The sheriff scowled, puzzled at this thought. Wrong? What was wrong? A middle-aged man, a young doll. You saw that every day. Funny though, she was young enough to be Duncan's daughter, and, yet it hadn't occurred to him at all that she might be.

Never occurred to him at all.

"What's in the county seat?" the girl said. And this meant he had to look at her again, and by now he could feel his eyes beginning to drool.

"Never mind, Milly," Duncan said. He gave the sheriff a flat, forced smile.

"No," Milly said. "I mean it. I want to know. What's in the county seat? Why do you have to take us there?"

The sheriff felt an unexplained urge to smile. There was something naive and childlike in the blonde's voice, but she was all woman and a perfect yard around in a couple of places. And she was over twenty, all right, because her little tummy had that loose round roll they begin to get when they spend a lot of time on their backs.

He kept his voice hard. He had to or he would begin to smile back at her, the way she kept giving him faint, tentative little smiles, like a kitten that wanted to be friendly and was just waiting for a friendly gesture in return.

"The county judge is in the county seat, m'am," Ben said. "I got to let him decide what to do about you folks."

"Why?" she said, protesting.

He exhaled heavily. "Because it beats me, that's why. You folks were hitting ninety — you know that? Gusts up to a hundred... Usually, I never stop speeders, but my God, you folks — "

"We're in a hurry," the blonde said, glancing through that rear window again. "Such an awful hurry."

"I believe that, all right," Ben said.

"Never mind, Milly." Duncan cleared his throat. His mouth was pulled in a way that made him appear to be smiling, even if he weren't always smiling with you.

"She is correct in one instance, officer. We are in a hurry... If there is any fine to pay — why, if you'll let us — "

"Yes." The girl leaned forward, smiling hopefully. "Let us pay the fine. Pay him, Harve, whatever it is, and — "

"Never mind, Milly — "

"I'm sorry. I don't set the fines." The sheriff shook his head. "I wouldn't know what to say in a case like this — a hundred miles an hour — geez."

The girl's eyes widened. "But, officer, we're on our way to — "

"Never mind, Milly."

"On your way to what?" Ben said, watching them.

"Tell him, Harve." Milly glanced through the rear window again.

Ben frowned. Now she had him doing it; he turned and took a quick gander down the heat-struck highway. He jerked his head back around.

"You tell him, Harve," the girl said again. "Maybe —"

"It's all right, Milly." The man sounded impatient and indulgent in the same breath; it was a neat trick. "I'll handle it...." He squinted, facing Ben through the window. "How far is it to the county seat, officer?"

"About fifteen miles back —"

"Fifteen miles!" It was a wail from Milly.

"Small town. You folks probably missed it, way you are traveling. Follow me."

He straightened, turning away.

"Officer," Duncan said. His mouth pulled, troubled. "We — we are in a hurry."

"You said that. Now if you'll just follow me back to Yeso Flats —"

"Look, officer. Sir. Please," the blonde called.

"Yeah?"

"Stay out of it, Milly," Duncan ordered.

"I can't. You won't tell him.... Please, officer, let us go. Just this once. I won't let him speed again. I promise —"

"Sorry, Miss —"

"Forget it, Milly. We'll just have to go back to Yeso Flats. You said Yeso Flats, officer? We'll have to go back and —"

"But we can't go back!" Milly cried out.

The sheriff bent forward and put both his hands on the window. He felt the shock of static electricity up his arms. He dropped his hands, wincing. This chick did the same thing to him. "Why can't you go back to Yeso Flats, miss?"

The girl's blue eyes clouded, and she looked as if she were about to say something, but a warning glance from Duncan stopped her.

She smiled in a wan way. "We're — on our way to be married," she said, making a sudden definite statement out of it, punctuated with a bright smile.

"Married?" the sheriff frowned.

Duncan attempted a smile. "That's right, officer. So you see, we are in a hurry."

The sheriff said, "You folks can get married back in Yeso Flats. The county judge there will likely perform the ceremony and take his fee out of your fine."

Duncan laughed in a flat way. "Well, I'm afraid that won't be possible," he said.

"Why not?"

"Well — " Milly was glancing through the rear window again.

"Never mind, Milly."

"Why not?" the sheriff repeated.

"We're on our way to get married, all right," Milly said, not looking at Duncan and blurting it out in one long breath, like a recitation she wasn't sure would be well received. "We are going to be married, but we've got to get to Mexico before we can do it. You see, I've got to get a divorce first."

5

Josh Carrdell returned through the lobby door to the deserted hotel's sagging veranda. He gripped powerful binoculars in his right fist.

He scowled, squinting against the white glare of the morning sun. Who'd be coming to Lust like this? And two cars? From two different directions? More traffic than any one week before in the past fifteen years.

He glanced about at the crumbling town and shook his head. His corduroy shirt, preserved and aged by sweat and dust, clung to his chest. His chest was boulder-thick and hadn't yet slipped past his solar plexus, despite the fact that he was pushing forty-five; he'd forgotten from which direction he was pushing it, because time didn't mean much up here.

He chewed his lip, giving a half-second of thought to time and its insignificance in a place like Lust. He shrugged. He supposed it was Thursday, but he wasn't sure; one day was like any other up here.

He rubbed the binocular lenses against his Levi's. His pants were salt gray and though they were much washed, often ripped, they were carefully patched. Carrdell was a man who had learned to exist without a woman in the desert and the mountains.

He strode across the loose boards, the gaping breaks in the veranda floor, passing the droop-bottomed cane rocking chair, to the only stretch of railing still standing intact between two-by-four supports.

Carrdell walked with the quick step of the desert man who has long ago learned that every move is a risk, and death is lurking as close as your next step. If a man stayed alive up here, he stayed alert. This movement was a natural part of him now, as it was in an Indian, deep and ingrained, so he stepped lightly without even thinking about it all any more.

His gaunt face was wind-cured and sun-dried, and he hadn't shaved for three days. He shaved only when his beard began to itch; then it became a necessity. A man didn't waste himself on non-essentials.

Through the glittering, haze-free clarity of the high country, he watched the two widely separated dust puffs.

Carrdell pressed the glasses against his eyes and first searched the mountains above him. There was just a mare's tail of dust showing up there; you might almost mistake it for a cloud, only he'd known it wasn't a cloud from the first instant. It moved, and glinted, and sometimes lost itself against the burnished gold of the aspens or the deeper green of the ponderosa pines up there, or showed itself above a boulder, or rode for a moment on a downdraft from the bald peaks, but always it moved downward toward him, as certain and truly as trouble itself.

Still, the wisp of dust up there was too far away for immediate concern, and he turned, placing the binoculars against his face again, fixing them on the larger dust cloud below him on the plain, fingering the adjustment, bringing the speeding car into arm's-length focus.

He stood motionless, watching the car and its lone occupant. At last, he whistled through his teeth. "It's a woman, George. And she's by herself."

The run-gaunted mongrel, curled in a swath of sunlight near the rocking chair, lifted its lean-nosed head enough to show fangs in a snarl. Otherwise it did not move.

"By God," Carrdell said. "It is a woman. Young. A looker. And she's headed straight up here."

The mongrel only tilted its head slightly, staring at Josh with something like contempt in its flat gray eyes.

The dog's wide skull was scratched and briar-slitted, and there were places along its back that had never regrown hair after he tangled with a wildcat. His fur was shabby, too, like a cheap coat that was being used as a make-do for one more season.

For some moments Josh went on staring at the car speeding across the plain, thousands of yards below him. And in all that flat brown and red and ash-gray country there, nothing else moved except that car and its plume of dust.

"Company," Carrdell said. "By God, George. Company."

The dog snarled but did not bother to lift its head again.

Carrdell stood on the porch, at the brink of the shade, the sun touching at his scuffed, dust-caked boots.

He estimated the distance to the car and the time it would require the woman to reach this high ledge from where she was on that wagon-track road down on Vandolo Plain. Though he could see her car and the dust, and the small patches of oak brush and mesquite thickets through which she traveled, she was many miles from Lust. Nobody, except hawks and buzzards, came up Burro Mountain any other way but following the winding trail.

Beyond her car, distantly, so it was almost lost to the naked eye, and would have been lost anywhere else except here where sunlight and thin atmosphere gave everything a terrible clarity, Carrdell could see highway 85 and black specks of cars. They were like addlepated ants, racing along the blue seam of roadway through mesquite and sage and flowering yucca.

From here he could see all that. But the few buildings that remained standing here in Lust—the four frame shacks along this row where he stood and the roofless adobe hut across the narrow street—none of these could be seen from the plain.

From down there one saw only the gradual rise to the base of the cliff and then the sheer, time-, wind- and water-eroded wall upward to the raised lip of the plateau. This huge ledge very gradually sloped from its edge, but the decline was enough so that not even the black roof of the two-story hotel could be seen from that plain. You came upon this abandoned town only after a tortuous, winding climb up the sloping east ridge of the mountain, and that road was pocked with holes and studded with outcroppings like slate spikes; nobody speeded along it for any appreciable length of time.

"Going down to the livery barn, George," Carrdell said over his shoulder.

He stepped out into the sunlight. He didn't bother to get his hat, but strode, lean and Indian-footed, along the hard white street past two askew frame shacks to the corner.

This main street led upward to the aspen and piñon forests and to the hog-back hills and peaks above him, but a smaller, less-used road turned left at the last shack and went past a frame barn that still had a roof and four sides intact and lost itself out in the sagebrush. A sign above the barn was still faintly legible: Livery Stable. This town had died before the first motor car had ever climbed this far.

Across the trail from the barn was empty, boulder-strewn mesa land, rising in undulating hillocks to the forests. He could remember when there had been other houses along this street, and the people who lived in them — the Pritchards and the Anthonys, the Gonzales and the Lowdermilks. They were long gone now, houses and people, along with every trace of them, and the land had reverted to oak brush and mesquite and prickly thorns, like a scraggly beard, to the timberline.

Carrdell scrubbed his hand across his jaw and pushed open the barn door. Inside, in the dimness, two burros stirred in their stalls. He walked past the fifteen-year-old jeep he'd bought from war surplus, scratched, battered, almost as evil-looking as his mongrel dog.

Just as the door swung closed, the dog lunged through the narrowing space.

"What do you want?" Josh said.

The dog showed his fangs, growling, and did not come near him.

Carrdell walked over to the stalls. He scrubbed his fist against the skull of the nearest burro. He glanced over his shoulder at the mongrel.

"You ever see anybody like George, Lincoln? How about you, Mary-Todd? You'd think anybody hates me the way George does, he'd stay away from me. Huh?"

The burros tilted their heads at the sound of his voice, and the dog snarled, watching them.

Hate. The thought association in this word clicked a switch in Carrdell's mind, filling it with a new set of pictures and thoughts. He scowled. "Say, you don't suppose that's Fran in that car, do you? She wouldn't be coming back up here? You think? Goddamn her. She better not. After the way she done me, the dirt." Then he shook his head. "Hell, what am I thinking about? That woman in the car was young. Young as Fran the last time I saw her… Not like she'd look now... Woman like Fran, why she's probably 97 percent vinegar by now.... Snarled worse than you do, George. By God, you think I'm pretty bad to live with. Hell, you oughta known Fran… By God, you ought to of been around here then, when I brought Fran up here... You'd see you got it pretty easy."

George tensed, back humping, hairs bristling. The sound George made between his fangs was almost a hissing.

"Ah hell. What do you know?" Josh said to the dog. He unbuttoned his shirt, pulled it off and hung it on a nail driven into a support.

He went to the water-trough then and pumped the hand pump until the trough was brimming full and spilling. Then he bent over it, scrubbing his chest and arms, neck and face, with a fat cake of tan kitchen soap.

He lifted his arms, scrubbing his armpits roughly for some moments.

He turned, dripping soap, glanced at the dog. "That was Fran. One thing. She never could stand underarm smell. Said it made her sick... She finally got to saying I made her sick… No matter what I did. No matter how hard I tried to please her... I'll tell you one thing, George, she was a bitch —"

George whined faintly, and Josh laughed in a cutting way. "I don't mean that kind of bitch, you stupid coyote."

George showed his teeth, snarling.

Soap dripping from him, Carrdell breathed in as deeply as he could, and then, sinking to his knees, plunged his body, all the way to his Levi's in the trough.

He fought, blowing and flailing under the water, until all the soap was washed away. George leaped back from his spray.

Carrdell stood up then, salt-brown hair plastered against his skull. He reached out, caught the sweat-streaked corduroy shirt and scrubbed his head and body with it, until the blood glowed under the surface of his sunburnt skin.

He got his razor out of the jeep, smeared his beard with soap, and shaved, staring at his dim reflection in the side-view mirror on the windshield.

George moved uncertainly toward the trough, then backed away, tail between his legs.

"Go ahead," Carrdell said over his shoulder. "It won't kill you. You look pretty sad yourself."

George looked up with an expression of malevolence in his face; then he moved forward cautiously, reluctantly and, with a rush, leaped into the trough.

The burros whinnied. Josh shouted at them. "Shut up, you jackasses. Shut up, Lincoln. Mary-Todd. I'll empty it."

George splashed around in the trough, keeping his head erect, swirling himself around, loosening the coated dust in the soapy water. Then he put his paws on the trough walls and leaped out to the straw-matted ground. He shivered a moment in a kind of chilled ecstasy and then shook himself dry.

Josh went on shaving and didn't even glance at the dog.

He finished shaving. He studied himself in the mirror a moment, then grinned. "Look ten years younger. Yep. Damned if I don't."

He put away the razor and rinsed his face under the mouth of the pump.

With one hand, his mind occupied with something else, he lifted the six-foot trough, spilling the water into a wooden gutter that carried it through a break in the wall to the yard.

He replaced the trough on its brick supports and pumped water again, until the trough was brimmed with clear, chilled water that smelled strongly of rotten eggs.

He hooked his wet shirt on his thumb, carrying it over his shoulder. He went out a rear door of the livery and crossed the field of mesquite, going under a cottonwood at the back door of the hotel.

When he came through the hotel front door a few minutes later, he was wearing a clean but faded denim shirt that fit like a layer of flesh over his bulging biceps and the thick muscles of his chest.

He had used military brushes on his short shock of hair, but it was drying now and beginning to spring upward and fall over his forehead.

He stood on the edge of the veranda. The dust wisp in the mountain had grown to a full-sized boll now, and he could hear the car from the plains struggling upward around the final rise before it came out on the plateau and entered the town limits.

6

Through the blurring haze of anxiety and exhaustion, Susan stared at the tumble-down cluster of shacks that appeared suddenly when her car rounded another snake curve and climbed one last knoll.

She exhaled, almost as if she'd been holding her breath in the endless climb from the plains below her. She saw now that she had come out on a huge shelf of land, an escarpment ripped out of the mountain by quakes and erosions a million years ago. The settlement had been built near its brink and beyond it a great meadow rolled upward to the timberline.

She lifted her foot from the accelerator. This was the place, this had to be the place, because she was too tired and too frightened, too exhausted to drive any further.

She looked about in a frantic way for a car, but found none. Wouldn't they hide a car, even up here? Then she saw the man standing, watching her.

She felt the trembling start deep in her stomach. She let the car slow, but kept it rolling forward. She passed the roofless adobe, and let the car roll all the way to the porch where the man stood.

She reached out, turned the switch, let the engine die.

For a moment neither she nor the man on the porch moved. Through her anxiety and weariness, she was aware of everything. The building where the man stood seemed to be the only one on the street in any kind of decent repair. One of its windows was boarded, blinds drawn, and it was covered with sacking. If anyone were going to exist in there, that window would have to be sealed against the bats, mosquitoes and deer flies. The other window, behind the man, still had its glass intact, unbroken. Three letters in old-fashioned scrolled printing remained on the glass, "H O T." She sighed. This was no lie. It was hot.

She gripped the steering wheel hard until the shaking in her stomach subsided. She opened the door then, still clutching the map, and got out in the white blaze of sunlight.

Beyond the man, an ugly mongrel roused itself growling, but the man gestured downward sharply. The dog sank again to the floor.

"Are — are you one of them?" Susan's voice sounded odd in her own ears.

Josh Carrdell hooked his thumbs in Levi pockets and stared at the girl. He whistled through his teeth. She was a looker, all right. In her early twenties. Lush, not really even ripe yet, though he bet she thought she was ripe. She had her beauty with her, and that was no lie. Fran was never like this, not even dressed up on Sunday; Fran could never touch this. These later models were real stoppers, all right.

"Am I one of what's?" he said, squinting.

She looked around helplessly. She was terrified that it was all some montrous mistake: this wasn't what she was looking for, it was all some fool's idea of a joke. There was no sign of a car. No sign of Matt. Nothing except this man, this unmoving wild man looking her over as if she were something to eat.

She felt, even through the fear and worry eating at her, that there was a film of unreality over this place, as if in some strange way it were gently haunted — not in the frightening sense of ghosts, but in evoked memories, the feeling that people were all around you in the odd sunlight. It was as if the silence up here was deeper than it was anywhere else, the heat more intense, and with the soft quality of forgotten places about it. You felt as if you should whisper so as not to rouse dead things better left sleeping. And there was the loneliness of a graveyard, the empty sense of loneliness, when you knew really and uncomfortably that you weren't alone at all.

"Come in out of the sun, m'am," Carrdell said. "Come up on the porch and set."

He nodded toward a dropped-bottom cane rocking chair.

She moved up on the narrow veranda out of the intense blaze of the sun. She looked at the chair but shook her head. "I'm looking for somebody — "

"I'm afraid there's nobody up here, m'am, but me and George. That's George there." The dog growled. "Don't mind George. George hates people. Me worse than most."

"You haven't seen anybody else?" Susan persisted. "You haven't seen a car? I don't know what color it would be — "

"We don't get many cars up this way — any color — "

"They were in a green one. I mean they started out in a green car, but they had it planned. They changed cars. The police found the green car a few minutes afterwards, and it didn't tell them anything. The green car had been stolen. They'd even stolen the car — "

"Sounds real interesting, m'am. Who? Who stole what?"

Susan frowned, almost frantic, staring at him as if truly seeing him for the first time. "Oh, I'm sorry. If you don't know anything about it, it must sound all mixed-up and confused. You must think I'm crazy ... and you'd be about right ... I'm nearly crazy... I'm worried sick... about my husband... he was shot and — I'll try to tell you about it. I'll try to make sense. My name is Susie Bishop — Mrs. Matt Bishop — "

"I'm Joshua Carrdell, Miz Bishop — "

"What?"

"Carrdell. My name is Carrdell. Josh Carrdell. Now you look in a pretty bad way. Why don't you set down there and rest a spell? Take it easy and tell me about it."

"You sure you haven't seen a car up here?"

"None except yours, Miz Bishop."

She sighed, seeming to sag inward, frustrated and helpless. "Oh, I might have known it. I don't suppose they even came this way at all."

"Who, Miz Bishop?"

She moved her head, looking about her again. "Well, you see

my husband — Matt Bishop — I told you, he works at the Yucca City National Bank — "

"That's a good hop from here. I was there once. Visited some people. Friends of my wife — "

"Your wife?" Susie grasped at this. "Is your wife here?"

He shook his head. "My wife left me, m'am, about fifteen years ago. She wanted me to live in a town — like Yucca City, or Santa Fe. I tried it. I made the effort. Then I brought her back up here with me, to do some prospecting. She couldn't stand this no more than I could tolerate living in Lordsburg. She left me."

"Oh." Susie sighed again. "My husband was a clerk in the Yucca City National Bank. Two men came in the back door early — it was Tuesday morning — this week. They forced past the officers and the clerks, and the guards in the vault and filled a suitcase with money. Then they took Matt — my husband Matt — as a hostage and forced the guard to open the front door for them, and the guard shot at them, but he didn't hit one of them — " her voice faltered, "he shot my husband."

"That's a tough break, m'am — "

"Yes. Well, they got away. Like I say, they changed cars. And they took Matt with them."

"And you asked was I one of them men?"

"I don't know. I'm half crazy, I know. I saw you standing here, like you were waiting for me — "

"I was, m'am. I dote on company. I tell you, I stay up here year on end seein' nobody, and it gets good to talk to folks."

"Oh, God."

"What?"

"I don't know why I'm here. I was a fool to think they would get word to me. Why would they bother? And how could they do it? You see, Mr. — "

"Carrdell. Josh Carrdell."

"You see, Mr. Carrdell, yesterday morning I found this map in a dirty envelope pushed under my front door." She opened it rapidly, her fingers trembling. She held it before them. "You see? You see right there? That black pencil ring. It — it is drawn around this place."

"Yep. Burro Mountain. You sure followed that map like a real prospector, m'am."

"When I saw it yesterday morning, I didn't know what to do. Then it seemed to me that maybe Matt was alive, but hurt, and maybe they would let me take him to a doctor if I would help them — I'd help them, no matter what they wanted me to do — if it would save Matt.... Maybe I was crazy, all the things I thought. But I had to come up here. Don't you think so?"

"Looks like the only chance you had, all right."

"Yes." She laughed, emptily. "That's what I thought. And then when I get here — I find nothing — just a ghost town in the mountains."

"Ghost town?" Carrdell laughed. "Why, m'am, you touch my civic pride. Why this here town is Lust, New Mexico."

"Lust?"

He laughed again. "That's right. Used to be quite a town. Quite a town. I was born here. Dying even then — the town was. It was drying up even then, but there was still several families trying to hang on, even when there wasn't nothing left to hang on for."

Susan glanced about her, feeling as if she were too tired even to walk back to the Dodge and start the long drive down the mountain. "You sure you haven't seen any other car, Mr. Carrdell?"

"They named this place Lust because that's what made it in the first place. Lust. The lust for silver, the lust for money, the — no, m'am, I ain't seen no other car.... I was out prospecting all yesterday.... Come in this morning, and I seen you down there on the plain, and then there was another car coming down from them mountains yonder."

Carrdell stretched his arm, pointing, and Susan turned, staring toward the distant timberlands and the peaks rearing beyond them. A blue Ford topped a rise, dust smoking and glinting above it.

They stood, silent, and watched the blue car race downhill toward them.

7

The blue Ford came into town fast from the north, a car on its way somewhere, with a driver who knew where he was going.

It raced all the way to the hotel before the big man at the wheel jerked hard right and stepped on the brakes, so it sidled in to the porch and stopped inches from the Dodge.

Two men got out of the car front, one from each side, coming around it, moving purposefully. This was business with them, and they were the businessmen with the know-how to handle it. The car was spattered with streaks of wet earth that told Josh Carrdell they'd fought a quicksand bog and won out. The fenders were dented and cactus needles had scratched long thin lines in the paint. They'd been in the desert and they'd been on the narrowest trails in the hills.

The two men converged on Susan; the taller, his face stark and white with rage, reached her first, moving with giant strides.

"You Bishop's wife?" he said to Susan, anger clipping his words short.

She nodded, staring up at the tall man, for the moment paralyzed with fear. It was as if she were looking at the devil himself. This man was so ugly, with high cheek-bones, sunken cheeks, deep-set eyes under black brows, and black hair that grew like horns from deeply indented temples. You almost expected him to say "Trick or treat," and pull off the mask. Only you knew it was no joking matter. This death mask of a face, with the rage in it, and the wildness in the deep-set eyes, was what this man had become in thirty-five years of living in evil.

Then she forgot to be afraid of the big man, forgot everything, except that if this man knew her, he knew Matt, and Matt must be in that car if he were alive at all.

"Matt!" she cried out.

She glanced up once more at the dark mask of a face and then twisted her body, moving around him. She ran toward the car.

"Matt!" she cried again.

The big man moved like a lynx, a mountain cat, faster than a cat, pouncing with no effort.

His hand flicked out, clawed her arm. Her head snapped on her shoulders as he jerked her around and away from the car.

"Matt's there," he said. "He's all right. For now. Nothing you can do for him. Not yet, and I want to talk to you."

Susan tried to writhe free of his clasp, gave that up.

"Talk to me?" She stared toward the back seat of the car. She couldn't see Matt. If he was there, he must be sprawled out on the back seat. "What about?"

She felt the thin hand tighten on her arm. She had never felt such strength in a man's hand. She felt her lower arm and fingers go numb. She felt helpless, dangling at the end of his arm.

The tall man accomplished what he wanted. She stopped staring at the car, tilted her head, looking up at him.

She shivered. There was murderous rage in this man's eyes. His mouth was lined in white, white rage.

He stared down into her face and jerked his head toward Josh Carrdell, without moving his gaze from hers.

"Who is this guy with you?"

"Name's Carrdell," Josh said.

"Shut up, Hicksville," the tall man spoke across his shoulder, spitting the words at Carrdell, "I'll get to you." He pulled his gaze back to Susan, staring down at her, his white-lined mouth twisted. "You bring him?"

"No!"

"You bring him?" The tall man's voice was quieter now, but there was rage quavering under it.

"I told you. No."

"And I tell you this." He bent that death mask closer. "I tell you this. We gave you credit for having sense enough to come up here by yourself. By yourself."

"I came alone. I didn't bring him!"

"He wasn't around here yesterday," the big man said. "We went through here yesterday. No sign of him. Nobody." He glanced over his shoulder. "That right, Poole?"

"That's right, Fletch. Looks like the chick is pulling one."

"Is that right, chick?" Fletch stared at her. "You ain't got sense enough to know you ain't hurting nobody but yourself when you try to queer us?"

Susan looked around, helplessly. Her gaze struck against the eyes of the younger man. Poole's eyes were climbing into bed with her. They were stripping her down, and digging into her.

Poole licked his lips. Medium height, he was heavyset, in his early twenties. His thick hair had a wave in it, and toppled over his forehead. His eyes were hotter and drier than the alkali dust of the street.

"Man," he said, licking his mouth again. "Man, you never know. You just never can understand, Fletch, how long seven years in the pen is until something like this — "

"You gone nuts, Poole?"

"Reckon I have. If flipping your bib over a doll like this is going nuts, then you better net me. Man why didn't you tell me?"

"Tell you what, Poole?"

"Why, man, why didn't you tell me that Bishop's wing was a lush cabbage? I'd of delivered that map in person Tuesday night — "

"God almighty." Fletch shook his head. "I'm damned if I can figure it. You go ape. You'd snarl up the whole deal for a quick snatch. I've worked with a lot of wrongos in my time, but you young kids — "

"Never mind me, Fletch. I ain't snarled up anything yet, have I? I'm just looking. She looks good, that's all."

Susan lurched free of Fletch's grasp, ran to the car. Fletch cursed Poole, heeled around, stalking her.

Carrdell took a step forward, but Poole's voice stopped him, contemptuous and cold. "Just stay where you are, Pop."

Susan wrenched open the rear door. Matt was propped up on the rear seat, head resting on a couple of folded army blankets. His shirt was caked with blood and he had both hands splayed across the bullet hole just inside his left pelvis bone.

"Matt. Oh, Matt."

She toppled against the black suitcase, struggling to reach him.

Only barely conscious, Matt turned his head. "Am I dreaming, baby?"

"Oh, Matt."

"Don't you worry, baby." His voice sounded weak, distant, as though across a bad connection. "You got — nothing to worry about — not any more."

"Oh, Matt — "

He tried to pull himself up, moving toward her, but he gasped, sucking in his breath and fell back on the blankets. He did not move.

Susan covered her mouth, screaming.

"It's all right, chick," Fletch said behind her. He caught her shoulders and forcibly pulled her away.

"He's dead," she whispered.

"He ain't dead. He's just passed out." He turned his head. "Come here, Poole. Let's get Bishop out of here where we can stretch him out."

Poole went around the car. He opened the door on the far side and crouched through it. He lifted Matt's legs while Fletch caught Matt's shoulders. They moved him off the seat and slowly eased him through the door to the ground.

Matt was still unconscious when they attempted to brace him against his feet long enough to get their shoulders under his arms.

"You'll — kill him," Susan whispered.

"Won't matter none to him, baby," Poole said out of the side of his mouth. "He's so near dead now he won't even know it."

"Shut up and let's get him out of the sun," Fletch said.

They were struggling to get grips on Matt's slumping body. Carrdell strode forward. He caught Poole by the arm and moved him aside as though Poole were a small boy.

"Get out of the way," he said.

He slipped one arm under Matt's shoulders, the other under his knees, swinging him up into his arms as he might a baby.

Fletch stepped back, watching, eyes cold. But he did not speak.

Carrdell strode across the veranda. He turned and spoke to Poole. "Open this door, kid."

Angered, Poole glanced at Fletch. The big man nodded.

Poole moved to the front door, opened it. Carrdell carried Matt inside. The others followed.

Susan was the last one to enter the hotel lobby. Except that the huge room was dry and dusty, it was in good repair. The ceiling of the lobby was the second story roof, beams exposed, brown with age. The second floor rooms were built along each side of the lobby and down a hall at the rear of it. A stairway led up to the second floor; a door below led to the downstairs back rooms and a rear exit. An old-fashioned semicircular desk still marked off a corner of the lobby.

Carrdell carried Matt to an old couch near the fireplace. He laid Matt on the couch, put his legs up.

Fletch followed him slowly across the room. Fletch leaned against the huge fieldstones of the fireplace watching Carrdell.

"Who are you, fellow? Where you come from?"

"He's just a man who lives here," Susan said from the door. "He doesn't know anything about all this."

"That's too bad," Fletch said. "He does now." He stared at Carrdell, still on his knees beside Matt Bishop. "You ever hear of Earle Fletcher, Carrdell?"

"No," Carrdell said. "Afraid not. Is that you?"

Fletcher seemed angered. "What you mean, you never heard of me?"

"Oh, for hell's sake, Fletch. A squaresville like him. What does he know?" Poole said.

Fletcher sighed. "Everybody knows about Earle Fletcher. Everybody. Look at me, Carrdell."

Carrdell turned, looking over his shoulder. "I see you."

"Look at me, Carrdell. Everybody ought to know the man that kills him."

"Why do you want to kill him?" Susan said.

"That's easy, chick. Real easy. The last thing we need is a witness." Fletcher's mouth pulled. "Besides, what difference does it make? We're going to do things my way. You might as well make up your mind to that."

As Fletcher spoke, Carrdell had turned again and was probing at the tender flesh at the bullet hole in Matt Bishop's side.

Susan moved slowly, woodenly, toward the couch, watching him. She was afraid to question him about Matt's condition. She was afraid of the answer.

As Carrdell worked, he began to speak across his shoulder. "Some fellows came up here. Three of them. They were tough cookies. You know why they were up here?" He didn't wait for an answer, his voice rode on smoothly. "They figured I had hit it big in uranium, They knew I had been prospecting these hills and if there was uranium up here, I'd have it. They moved in, these boys. They were going to take what I had. But it didn't go their way. Just didn't happen. I had to work on them three boys. Took 'em apart. Limb from limb."

"Sure, Pop," Poole said. "You're a big man."

"Shut up, Poole," Fletcher said. "Let him have his say. I love to hear these farmers tell about what big men they are. Hell, I had bigger men than him cleaning my shoes. Me. Earle Fletcher. You hear that, mud eater?"

Cardell shrugged. He turned, giving Fletcher an empty grin.

"Go ahead. Grin." Fletcher went cold. "Have fun, hick."

"For hell's sake, Fletch," Poole said. "Let's finish him now. Let me do it."

"The kid's right," Carrdell said in a taunting tone. "Like them three fellows I'm telling you about. They talked about it too much."

Fletcher's face remained cold. "You saying I talk too much, Carrdell?"

"Fletch, give me the word." Poole was trembling with rage. "I'll take care of him."

Fletch lifted his hand, motioning Poole to wait. "You saying I talk too much, Carrdell?"

Carrdell shrugged. "I was telling you the fault of them three fellows, that's all. They should have been smarter. They should have known if they didn't shoot me in the back, they were lost."

Poole's voice shook. "I won't shoot you in the back, big man. Get up. Turn around. I want you to see it."

Caudell went on talking toward Fletcher, grinning, ignoring the boy. "Like I say, the man that don't strike at the right time don't get to strike at all. And anyhow, you boys ought to give me credit for being at least half as smart as guys that have spent any-way seven years behind bars — isn't that what you said, boy?" He glanced at Poole. "You been seven years without a woman?"

"What's it to you?" Poole said. He glanced at Susan, licking his lips and grinning. He moved toward her. "I can have a woman now — any time I want her."

Susan shuddered. "You're an animal." She retreated a step. "Stay away from me — you animal."

"Don't call me no animal," Poole yelled at her. "I'm just as good as you are, doll. Better!"

"You're an animal," Susan said again, staring at him. "A dirty animal."

Poole stepped toward her, fist raised to backhand her across the face. He stopped suddenly, only a few feet from her. He laughed at her, a sharp and bitter sound. Something was suddenly extremely amusing to him; he had his private joke and she was the butt of it. His mouth twisted, and he glanced at Matt prostrated on the couch.

"I'm an animal, huh, baby? Well, tell me this. If I'm such an animal — what does that make *him?*" He spat toward Matt.

Susan shook her head, her face white. She stepped back again. Poole laughed, advancing toward her, sensing the smell of fear about her now, mixed with the other good smells of her that distracted and roused him.

"What do you want with us — Matt and me, and with him — " Susan nodded toward Carrdell. "You used Matt to — to rob that bank — why are you keeping him?"

"Keeping him?" Poole said. "Boy. How about that, Fletch? We're keeping poor ole Matt Bishop — "

Fletcher was frowning, head cocked as if listening for something. He turned, eyes chilled. "Look, girl. Why don't you just figure we got our reasons why your husband is still with us and let it go at that? We also got our reasons why we got you up here. Now don't push it."

Poole laughed. "That's right, baby. Let's you and me get to know each other. We ought to be real good friends. We're in this together like we are." He reached for her.

Earle Fletcher raised his hand and leaned forward, poised, listening.

"Hold it. Wait, Poole. There's a car out there. Somebody is coming up here."

Carrdell grinned, pushing away from the couch and getting lithely to his feet. "You got pretty good hearing for a stir bum, Fletcher. Why I didn't hear that car myself more than ten minutes ago."

But Fletcher's cold gaze was fixed on Susan. "I knew your place was watched. Maybe a guard on you. That was a chance I took. But, baby, if you led some cop up here, I'm really going to fix you."

Poole ran to the door.

Fletcher said, "Wait a minute, Poole. Take it easy. Back up over there away from that door, and let's see who's in that car."

Both men drew guns from shoulder holsters and moved into the deepest shadows and stood silently, watching that front door.

8

"Three cars in one day!" Carrdell's voice had awe in it. "What do you know about that?"

"Shut up," Fletcher ordered from beside the glass window.

"Why, a man can get mighty lonesome up here — " Carrdell said.

"I said, shut up." Fletcher was pressed against the wall, watching the car move along the street outside. "Shut up. You make one wrong move and I put a bullet in you. I got nothing to lose now."

They heard the car stop outside at the front porch. The dog was barking, its raging vibrating through the building.

"Stop that damned dog," Fletch said.

"Now George," Carrdell said, "he don't like company as much as I do. George has got a thing about people. He hates people. Even strangers."

Carrdell glanced at Fletcher and Poole as he strode across the lobby. "George is funny about strangers. Hates them right on sight — worse than he hates folks he knows."

"Shut up and stop that dog." Fletcher spat the words at him.

Carrdell hesitated, eyes changing suddenly. He stared at Fletcher.

"You get rid of those people," Fletcher said. "Get them out of here. Fast."

Carrdell didn't glance toward Fletcher again. He nodded, threw open the hotel door, yelling to make himself heard above the barking. "Shut up, George. You want me to kick you across the next reservation?"

He walked out on the porch.

Poole said, "What's he pulling, Fletch?"

Fletcher gestured downward sharply. "Forget it. I can see him. Anything he does. Right through this window."

When Carrdell stepped out on the porch, the mongrel subsided, but remained poised, snarling at Carrdell as if he'd attack him if Carrdell ever turned his back.

Harvey Duncan stepped out of his Cadillac. There was a hissing sound from beneath the front hood. It sounded as if one of the puncture-proof tires had a hole in it.

Duncan stood staring helplessly at the pink radiator. "Boiling," he said to Carrdell. "Can you tell me, my good man, where is the nearest garage?"

"Auto mechanic?" Carrdell shook his head. "Nearest one is Yeso Flats."

"Yeso Flats?" Duncan said. "Yeso Flats. Christ."

Milly got out of the car and came around it. "What's the matter, Harve? What did the man say?"

"The man said Yeso Flats," Duncan told her. "That's all he needed to say to me. Christ. Yeso Flats."

"What's at Yeso Flats?" Milly said. "Except the county judge? I know the county judge is at Yeso Flats."

"Christ," Duncan said. "They charge you almost ten grand for a goddamn car, and the goddamn thing runs hot the first hill it climbs."

"Take it easy, Harve," Milly said. "Please take it easy. You know what the doctor said to you."

Harve jerked his head around. "What about the doctor?"

"Well, now, Harve. Don't get excited. I don't know what the doctor said to you. I only know he said something that had you awfully worried."

"I wasn't worried. Now will you forget that damned doctor?"

Milly tried to smile. She looked around helplessly. "What are we going to do, Harve?"

"How in hell should I know what we are going to do?"

But Milly was staring round-eyed, open-mouthed, at the tilting, crumbling buildings. "Why, Harve, this isn't a town. This place is — falling down." She turned, frantic, looking at Carrdell. "What kind of place is this?"

"It's a ghost town, Milly," Duncan said, staring at the steaming Cadillac.

"A ghost town?"

"This is Lust," Carrdell said.

Milly blinked. "What?"

"That's the name of the town," Carrdell said. "Lust. Lust, New Mexico."

"Lust," Milly said, smiling. She looked around again. "What a cute idea. Lust. Sounds like a wonderful place for us to spend our honeymoon, Harve."

"I'm glad you're pleased," Duncan said.

"You folks just married?" Carrdell said.

"Well, we — " Milly began.

"Yes." Duncan broke across her words. "Yes. We were just married.... Do you happen to know anything about cars?"

Carrdell shrugged. "Enough to keep one running. Looks to me like you got a broken radiator hose, or water pump trouble. Or maybe — if you're lucky — your water just boiled out."

"Well, we got to get out of here as soon as we can," Duncan said, glancing at the sun.

"Is there any place we can get anything to eat?" Milly said.

Duncan's voice was sharp. "You see any place, Milly?"

She shrugged and laughed. "Well, I'd even settle for a ghost-burger."

Duncan stared at Milly a moment as though he had never seen her before. Then he shrugged. "Be my guest."

He turned his back on her.

"Don't be mad at me," Milly said to his back. "This never would have happened if you hadn't taken that road down there. I told you it didn't go anywhere — "

He heeled around. "Milly, stop it. We've been through that. Now the map showed a road leading south — unimproved, but all the way from 85 south to another highway."

"I got bad news for you, mister," Carrdell said. "This road just plain stops. Three or four times. Of course you can make it all the way through — "

"You see," Duncan said to Milly.

" — on a horse," Carrdell finished.

Duncan exhaled heavily. "All right. So I made a mistake. Sue me. Line up the firing squad." He stared hard at Milly. "It's not the first mistake I ever made in my life."

"Why don't you folks come in," Carrdell said. "You'd be mighty welcome. I'd be pleased to feed you. Let your car cool off and we'll take a look at it."

Milly was already moving across the porch.

Duncan said, "Wait a minute, Milly — "

"What for?" she stared across her shoulder. "He said he'd feed us, didn't he? That's good enough for me."

She strode through the doorway, and George followed at her heels.

Carrdell smiled, looking at Duncan. "Look at that George. He's plumb taken with that wife of yours. Reckon he never smelled anything smells that good. Quite a fine looking lady. Yes, sir. Used to be quite a few like her around here when Lust was in its prime."

"Yes," Duncan said. "I imagine so."

Milly screamed and came stumbling back through the door. Her eyes were round now, and her hand was pressed against her mouth. George had to leap out of the way to keep from being stabbed by her high heels.

"Harve!" Milly screamed. "There are men in there. With guns!"

Duncan didn't even look astonished. He exhaled heavily. He glanced at the other two cars parked outside the old hotel and shrugged. "It figures," he said. "We got to get out of here, Harve," Milly cried.

Earle Fletcher appeared in the doorway, the gun in his hand. "Come on in, folks." His voice was low. "Like Carrdell says, you're real welcome."

Duncan stared at the gun in Earle's hand. Then he pulled his gaze to Josh Carrdell and looked him over. There was not the faintest trace of fear in Duncan's face.

"What kind of hold-up deal is this?" he said to Carrdell.

"I can't answer that," Carrdell said. "This here is my place, but —"

"But I'm running it right now," Earle Fletcher said. "So you folks come on in. Nice and easy. Like I say." Fletcher stepped aside and watched them troop past him, Milly first, arms folded under her lush breasts as if she were carrying an armload of something. Carrdell was next with George beside him. Duncan walked in slowly, nostrils distended, looking the place over.

Fletcher spoke to Duncan. "You don't happen to be a doctor, do you?"

"No. I'm not."

"I heard your lush say something about a doctor, outside," Fletcher began.

"He went to a doctor. The doctor told him something and he won't tell me what it was," Milly said.

"I'm all right, Milly," Duncan said. He looked Fletcher over with contempt and distaste in his face. "What do you felons want with us?"

"You're in no spot to talk down your nose at me, friend," Fletcher said. "Why don't you just take it easy? Me and Poole will make the decisions."

Duncan stared at him a moment, shrugged. He walked away from him.

He stopped, staring down at Matt, unconscious on the couch. His head jerked up. He looked at Fletcher and Poole, then brought his gaze back to Susan, who was crouched on the floor beside Matt's head.

"This man's been shot," he said.

"How about that?" Poole imitated Duncan's tone. "This is the kind of man I like. The big shot. No wonder he can buy big cars. Huh, Fletch? Here's a man who sees things fast. Things nobody else sees. Looks at something. And makes the quick decision. Bullet hole in the guy. Blood all over every thing. And right away he spots it. This man's been shot."

9

Milly sank into an overstuffed chair near the couch. Dust clouded up around her. She waved her hand in front of her face and tried to blow it away.

Poole heeled around, facing Fletcher. "We fooled around long enough, Fletch. The woman is here. We got what we want. Let's get out of here."

Susan's head came up. "You can't move Matt. You'd kill him if —"

Poole laughed. "Who said anything about moving him, doll? If we just move you, that's good enough for me."

"Always got your mind on dames," Fletch said. "Wonder you ain't gone out of your head over this new one."

Poole laughed. "Yeah. She's carrying a crate of goodies right in front, all right." He stared at Milly, moving his gaze over her. "Her kind's all right — for guys like you, Fletch — and maybe for the old gent she brought with her. I guess when a guy gets your age — his age — you get to wanting something like that — maybe when your time's running out, and you think you won't get any more... . But me? I like the sweet and soft-looking kind. Gentle-looking little dolls, huh! Kind of remind me of my mother... . Huh! I wanta smash my fist right in their face and rip their clothes off them."

Fletch replaced his gun in its holster. He glanced at Poole, shook his head. "Trouble with you is, Poole, you're sick. You don't never really want nobody unless you can hurt 'em some way ... You're gettin' even. Everything you do, you're gettin' even with somebody."

"Lay off me, Fletch. I been with you. Since the day we broke out. I done everything you done. Right along with you. I been as good as you. All down the line. Don't you forget it."

Earle Fletcher laughed. He paced back and forth across the lobby, watching the sun-stricken street through the open doorway. He was scrubbing his hands together.

He was thinking of something else, trying to work his way out of this newest turn in the maze in which he found himself trapped. His voice was soft, distant, his mind only partly occupied with the things he was saying.

"Trouble with you, Poole. You're still just a kid. You don't know nothing yet."

"I've sided you, Fletch. All the way."

Earle Fletcher made a downward gesture toward the boy. "I don't know. This place. Gives me the creeps. I felt that, yesterday when we was through here. I get in a place and I don't like it. Nothing I can explain. It's something in my bones. I been big on instinct. All my life. I get a feeling about something — even when I can't understand it, or explain why I feel a certain way, there it is. That feeling. It's kept me alive a long time. I've seen a lot of guys. A lot of big ones in my time. They've come along, and they got pretty big. But something happened to them. And they're gone, and I'm still here. Me. Earle Fletcher. I grew up in Brooklyn. Brownsville. They was a lot of tough guys in that town. Some of the guys I met since then, I wouldn't spit on. I could look and I could know when they was weak, or would fold when it got bad. You ain't like that. I give the check from the first — you got the guts, all right. But you better make up your mind to one thing. I know when a thing's wrong... . And that's right now.... When the Feds got me, I did time. First time. Only time. And they couldn't hold me... . Just the same, I knew then. This instinct I had ... Something was wrong. It bugged me. I couldn't figure what it was. It was them finking Feds... . Getting at me through a dame... . a no-account, two-bit dame. I'm telling you. You lay off these dames. We get out of this, I'll buy you dames by the dozen ... swell dolls ... babes that wouldn't use the same powder room with these bags."

"I'm with you, Fletch. You know that. Right down the line. What we going to do?"

Fletcher paused, looking around the dusty room with the unreality seeming filtered into it on the dust-ridden sunlight. He shook his head, frowning. "Something is wrong, kid. Bad wrong. First, it was stopping to try to get that stupid country doctor to get the bullet out of Bishop....I knew it was wrong....I knew it. That lousy son, calling the cops.... Then them patrol cars, crowding us... roadblocks... pushing us back up in here...." He shivered. "I don't like this place."

"They ain't gonna take us up here, Fletch."

Fletcher laughed, a chilled sound. "Nobody is going to take me. But I got to figure. I got to think. I got to figure where we gone wrong.... How we can make it out of here."

"Fletch, we ought to hit the road. I can tell you that. *I* got that feeling."

Fletcher stared at him, face cold. "Hit the road. Where? Roadblocks on every highway? Let me alone. Let me think about it. I'll tell you when."

He turned and strode through the door, going out into the sunlight. He slammed the front door behind him.

Poole, his young face troubled, ran across the room to the dust-smeared front window, and stood staring through it, watching Earle Fletcher out in the ghost-town street.

Carrdell went back to the couch and sat on the rolled arm of it, at Matt's feet. He stared at the blood-caked shirt, but did not say anything. He moved his gaze, watching Susan smooth Matt's hair back from his face.

Harvey Duncan pulled off his coat, folded it and tossed it across the desk top in the corner near the stairs. He breathed out heavily, loosening his tie and running his fingers inside his collar.

"Hot," he said. He moved over to the fireplace, staring at the gray ashes in it, a log only partly burned away, black and charred, and cold.

"Yes. Days are pretty hot up here," Carrdell said. "We get blasts right off the desert. But the nights are cold. Wind seems to come right through those boards."

Duncan nodded toward Poole, leaning against the window frame. "How long do you think they'll keep us here?"

"I don't know," Carrdell shook his head. "I don't know what that Fletcher has got in his mind.... You couldn't know. He don't even know yet.... You can tell one thing, though. The cops chased him, pushed him up here in these hills, and now he don't know how to get out."

"He looks like the kind of rat that's been pushed into a lot of corners in his time," Duncan said. "Earle Fletcher. I've heard that name.... He was on top of the FBI most-wanted list one time. A real big-shot hood back East."

"He scares me," Milly said. "He scares me when I look at him."

"Right there is a first," Duncan said. "I never knew any man could scare you."

"Don't try to be nice to me, Harve," Milly said in what she felt was a heavily ironic tone. "Don't blame me for all the bad things that have happened."

"I don't blame you, my dear," Harve Duncan said. "I'm quite willing to take the blame for everything — to myself. I wanted you. And I got you. I'm not blaming anybody."

"You have such a lovely way of saying things," she pouted.

"You folks sure you're on your honeymoon?" Carrdell said. He sighed. "I recall Fran and me. We — even we got along better than this — the first three or four weeks."

Duncan smiled in that odd way that might have a dozen different meanings. "Don't misunderstand me. No. Milly's a wonderful girl. Young. And — wonderful. Everything about her is wonderful. My trouble is that — well, let's face it, when a man is fifty-two and his car radiator starts boiling, and the thermometer hits a hundred and two in this shade, and a cop fines him seventy-five dollars for speeding on a wide open, flat, stupid highway, and then he takes a wrong turn and is too stubborn to admit it and turn around, the tensions pile up in him. A man fifty-two isn't as resilient as a young man might be.... It's hard for me to bounce back. To be a nice guy...." He tried to smile, looking at Milly. "I'm sorry. I hope you can forgive me."

"It's all right, honey. I know how you feel."

"Do you?"

There was something in his tone that irritated Milly. She snagged at it, crying out. "There you go, Harve. You're always running me down. You're so sarcastic. You act like I'm — well, stupid, like I can't understand anything. I — I understand. You're tired. And hot. And worried. I understand. You got a lot to worry about, all right.... We don't even know where Reed is."

"Oh for God's sake, Milly," Harve said. "I'm not worried about Reed. Will you get that through your head for once and all?"

"Well, I think you're worried about him — "

"Milly!"

"You act like you're worried about Reed. You never mention him. But you act like it."

Duncan paced back and forth before the large fireplace as if consciously controlling his emotions, counting to a million by tens.

Finally he shrugged, glancing at Carrdell still perched on the couch arm, watching them with avid interest, the perfect host. He spoke to Carrdell, but actually was talking to himself, speaking aloud.

"I don't know if it ever really works."

"What, Harve?" Milly said, leaning forward. "You don't know if what works?"

Duncan was staring at the backs of his hands, talking to them. "I don't know. A man my age. A girl twenty-two. I don't know. It's like trying to press two whole different worlds into the same world — "

"Why, I'm happy with you, Harve. You know I've been."

"Have you? Maybe I've been happy, too. I suppose I've been happier these past few months with you than I'd ever been in thirty years before that. I worked hard all those years. I had a wife at home, and when I went there she was always there, and polite, and seemed pleased to see me again. She had parties and I attended them. I needed a nice dinner for a client, and she saw that it was perfect. But sometimes, for weeks, it was almost as if we weren't aware of each other at all. Then when she died and I was alone, it was as if I'd been speeding along in a car at sixty miles an hour and suddenly changed gears, throwing the thing into reverse, stripping the gears. The habits of my whole life were abruptly changed. I looked around, and I wondered what had become of the Harvey J. Duncan I once had known. I was getting old, and I had lived this polite, dull routine existence in a rut. I had missed my youth, my young manhood, all the good years, and here I was about to miss life itself."

He strode back and forth, the smile gone, his face troubled. "I didn't know what I wanted. I didn't know what to do. I'd wake up, alone, in the middle of the night, and I'd actually be sweated, and scared. And the only way I would go back to sleep at all was to lie there with the lights on."

Carrdell smiled, nodding. "And then you met Milly here. Why, that sounds fine."

Duncan glanced up, as if aware of Carrdell suddenly. He gave him a brief smile, nodded. "Oh, yes. That was fine."

Milly laughed. "I was in this bar. It was really a nice place. Finest in town. I mean, Reed didn't mind me going into a bar alone for a drink in the afternoon. I mean, you know, if I went into the best places, he didn't mind."

"Reed?" Carrdell prompted her.

"My husband," Milly said. "I met Duncan and he was so nice. Pretty soon I was seeing a whole lot of him. I mean, well, he was so nice and understanding, and I was so miserable — and unhappy —"

"With Reed?" Carrdell prompted her again.

"Oh, yes. Just miserable. Reed just kept me sick and unhappy all the time. And here was poor Harve, had lost his wife. He had his grief, and I could cheer him up. And he just did me worlds of good. It was like we were fated to meet — you know — like it was meant to be.... I felt that way, right from the first, didn't I, Harve?"

"That's what you said." Harve breathed out deeply again, leaning against the fieldstone.

Milly gave Carrdell a fleeting, uncertain smile. "When I knew that Harve and I were right for each other, like we were intended and all, I wanted to divorce Reed right away. But Reed was so rotten about it. Like the way we fought. Like cats and dogs, like I said to Reed, we just fight like cats and dogs. Looked like he would want to get a divorce. But he was just terrible about it.... Why, one afternoon he came home when Harve was there visiting me — perfectly respectable and formal and everything, why Reed just raged. He was going to kill poor Harve if he ever came near me again.... So, there wasn't anything for Harve and me to do, and I agreed to run away with him to Mexico where I could get a divorce and we could be married."

Carrdell nodded, pleased. "So. That's what you did?"

"We — we're on our way there," Milly said.

10

"Susie...."

Susan jerked her head up as if brought out of a stupor by the sound of Matt's agonized whisper.

She stared at his face. He rolled his head. His face was twisted in a pained way, and he was whimpering almost like a small boy. She must have fallen half asleep, leaning against him, drugged by fatigue and anxiety.

Drowsily, she looked around, as if trying to remember where they were. And then the recall was total, and abrupt. She pressed her hand against Matt's fevered face, trembling.

"Matt." She looked up at the people in the room — Poole near the window, the blonde woman in the old chair beside her, Duncan in his shirt sleeves before the fireplace. She brought her gaze back to Carrdell. The prospector. Oh God, if any of these people could help her....

"He's conscious, Mr. Carrdell," she whispered, frantic. "Matt's conscious ... Isn't there anything we can do for him?"

Carrdell had been staring at Harvey J. Duncan and the blonde woman in admiration and pleasure. He was pleased to have them up here. They were his kind of people, all right. He had always admired strong people, who did what they wanted to do, who took what they wanted, and to hell with the rest of the world. The hell even with what other people think. A man had to be bold if he really found anything in this life that was worth while.

He slid off the arm of the couch and knelt beside the troubled young wife. He laid his hand on her shoulder, feeling the way she was trembling. She did not withdraw from him. She trusted him; she needed his help. It disappointed him faintly that she trusted him so implicitly. That certainly wasn't the greatest compliment a woman could pay a man, not even a woman as young and as troubled as little Mrs. Bishop. He wasn't that old. He looked pretty good, in a fresh shirt and shaved, and all.

"We'll do what we can, m'am," he said.

He bent forward, examining the bullet wound in Matt's side.

Proud flesh. It was getting worse all the time, like venison left too long in the sun. He wasn't confident about what they could do.

"We'll sure do what we can, don't you worry," Carrdell said again. This was the least he could do for her.

"Susie — "

"I'm here, Matt...." She stroked his forehead. She felt as though her hand were burning.

"Did ... I ... ever tell you about Jake, Susie ...? Did I ever tell you?"

"Rest, Matt. Please..."

"I got to talk about Jake, Susie... I never told nobody. But you... I never did... Jake didn't steal those tires, Susie..."

"Oh God, Matt, what are you talking about?"

Cardell patted her shoulder. "Take it easy, Miz Bishop. He's out of his head with the fever. He's rambling ... He don't know what he's saying.... He don't even know where he is."

Susie crumpled, pressing her head against Matt's shoulder, crying deep inside herself, her body shaking. She did not make a sound.

"Jake... was a Jew boy... Susie... I was his only friend... I liked Jake... I really did... I liked him ... We got along swell... His folks were good to me... But when they blamed him for stealing those tires... I didn't say anything. They wanted to believe Jake did it. Jake's father was making money — and the rest of the people in town weren't — and all they wanted to do was hurt Jake's father... any way they could... They said Jake stole those tires... But Jake didn't do it. Oh God, Jake didn't do it... And, I think... I think they knew he didn't... They — even knew that I did it... They knew it, but they kept saying Jake did it... Even cause that's what they — wanted to believe... Even Jake's father — Jake's father knew I did it... even when he couldn't prove it... The way he looked at me, Susie... Nobody ever looked at me like that... Oh God, Susie... I couldn't tell anybody... The best friend... My best friend, Susie... that's what I did to him."

Susie clutched his shoulders in her hands. "Please, Matt. It's all right... Don't torture yourself any more."

Carrdell drew her away gently. "It's all right, Miz Bishop. He don't know... He's out of his head... He don't know."

She turned around on her knees, catching at Carrdell's arm, searching his face. "Can't we do something? Can't we get him to a doctor?"

The front door had opened and Fletcher stepped through it. He glanced at Poole, and then stood listening to Susan.

He spoke coldly. "Nobody is going nowhere, chick ... not till I say so."

Susan turned, still on her knees, still clinging to Carrdell's arm. Through blurring tears she stared at Earle Fletcher, but there was no way to reach him, nothing she could say that would touch him. She sagged, frustrated, and turned her face back to Carrdell. "Please," she whispered. "Do something. Please."

"We'd have to get that bullet out."

"Please try — "

"I better tell you. I'm no doctor. I've taken bullets out of men. Some of them survived it... not all of them.... It ain't like you think... the shock is bad, sometimes the shock kills them when the bullet don't ..."

"He'll die," she whispered.

"It's up to you, m'am. I'll attempt it if you say so. I just want to warn you. It's going to be rough . .. not impossible, maybe... but mighty rough."

"If there's anything I can do to help," Duncan offered.

"Or me," Milly said. "One thing. The sight of blood don't make me faint. I get a little woozy. But I don't faint. I'd like to help."

Carrdell nodded. "All right. Once I saved an Indian that had shot himself with a poison arrow. His own poison arrow. He'd poison-tipped it to kill some coyotes, you know, and shot himself. In the foot — "

"Please," Susan whispered, her voice frantic.

Carrdell nodded again and stood up. "You'll have to forgive me, m'am. I have so little company like this, I get started talking and can't stop.... Well, first thing, we better have some boiling water."

"What for?" Milly came around the couch and joined him.

Carrdell stared at Milly a moment, then shrugged. "I'm damned if I know," he said. "But they always do it. Minute a man is hurt, somebody boils some water." He took her arm and led her through the rear door, still talking. "I got an old wood stove back here. Maybe you and Harve can fire it up and boil some water."

"All right, Harve said. He followed them.

They went along the musty hallway. Carrdell said, "If we can't think of anything else to use the boiling water for, we can make us some coffee. I got some coffee back here, and all of you folks looked famished. Coffee won't hurt none of us. I want you all to have a pleasant stay while you're here with me."

Ten minutes later, Carrdell returned to the hotel lobby carrying a pint bottle of whisky, an Indian herb remedy in a quart Mason jar and two sharply honed knives. He made a small hook in the end of a length of bailing wire.

"This is it. This ought to do it," he said. He glanced at Susan. "Don't you worry. We'll have boiling water, and I'll get that bullet out. You just hang on. You just pray."

Poole and Fletcher moved in from the door. They stood at each end of the couch, like pallbearers, watching Carrdell as he knelt over Matt and cut away the bloodclotted shirt.

Carrdell spoke soothingly to Susan. "Don't fret, m'am. If it gets too hard to bear, you take a nice long pull on this here whisky. Don't worry about your husband. He don't feel nothing.... Take my word for that."

Susan stood straight, hands clenched at her sides. Her eyes were closed. She did not speak aloud. She may have been praying.

Duncan and Milly returned through the rear door then. Duncan's shirt and face were streaked with soot. He said, "We got the fire started and the water on—"

And then he stopped talking, staring beyond them at the man standing in the front doorway.

Puzzled, Milly looked up at Harve and then followed the direction of his gaze. She pressed her hand against her mouth, screaming. "Reed," she cried out.

"Yes, baby, it's me," Reed said in the doorway. His face was pale, tormented. He tilted the hock-shop gun in his fist. "Didn't you know I was going to find you two lovebirds, baby? Didn't you know I was going to find you and kill you?"

II

For a breathless moment, the gray lobby resembled a still life done in surrealistic style and caught in a wormwood frame. In this strangely, yet gently illumined room, the people were not people at all, but unmoving objects caught in odd positions.

Poole and Fletcher were tensed, half-turned, at each end of the old couch. Both had been thrusting hands inside coats for automatics holstered there. Now both paused, waiting.

Their faces were gray. Reed Hall, standing armed in the doorway, had the youthful, harried look of the crew-cut Fed. At first sight both Poole and Fletcher were ready to start shooting at him. If Reed had not spoken so abruptly, so bitterly to Milly and Harvey Duncan, either Poole or Fletcher would have killed him before he could have taken one more step forward.

Neither Duncan nor Milly moved. It was as if each had suspended breathing, gazes fixed on the gun in Reed's fist.

After an unbearably long time, Carrdell stood up, rising slowly, cautious to make no overt move that might trigger Reed Hall's taut-strained muscles.

He moved unhurriedly around the couch. He was smiling, and at the same time was watchful.

"Stay where you are," Reed said. Shadows swirled deep in his eyes; a man who detested violence was caught and trembling with the violence in him.

"Friend — " Carrdell's voice was level.

"Stay where you are." Reed's sick green eyes barely touched at Carrdell, darted back to Milly and Harvey Duncan beyond the couch. "I don't want to hurt you, mister. I got no quarrel with you. Just don't try to stop me."

Carrdell continued moving toward Reed, light-stepping on the balls of his feet, but not hurrying it.

"I'm not trying to stop you," Carrdell said. "But I just thought I better tell you — "

"Yeah?" Reed jerked his head, glancing at Carrdell, then looked back at Harvey and Milly, as though he expected them to evaporate like cigarette smoke before his very eyes. "Yeah? Tell me what?"

"I figured I better tell you. Way you walked in here now — like this — with that gun drawn — you nearly got yourself killed — by Mr. Fletcher there." Carrdell moved his head, indicating the tall thin man, and moved it again toward the younger felon. "Or by Mr. Poole over there... or by me."

Reed shivered visibly. A muscle worked at the corner of his mouth, but the lines deepened about his nostrils. What difference did it make, the manner of his death? Did these characters think they could hurt him after what Milly and her over-age lover boy had done to him?

"I don't give a damn." Reed's voice was sharp. He glanced at Fletcher, Poole, raked his gaze across Carrdell, but moved it always back to Milly's face. "Don't think you can scare me, mister. What in hell would I care if you guys shot me?" He shook his head, staring at his wife and Duncan. "What's there to live for in this damned fouled-up world — when men like him!" he spat toward Duncan," — when men like that walk off with the woman you love — the woman you are married to?"

In the moments since Reed had walked through that front door, Milly had suffered shock, astonishment, and an instant of fear. But now it had all dissolved, and when she looked at Reed, she didn't see a dangerous man with a gun in his hand, she saw only the mild, sweet man she'd been married to all these years. A man who shuddered when he stepped on a cockroach.

Milly moved forward. Duncan lifted his hand, trying to touch her arm, hoping to restrain her, but she stepped around him. She knew Reed so well, she had known him for so long, she knew so much about him, all about him; she could not remain afraid of him, even when he clutched a gun in his fist, and waved it, trembling with rage.

There was even faint exasperation and impatience in her voice. "Well, Reed. Aren't you happy? Making a scene like this? My goodness, Reed. We went through all this. In the privacy of our own bedroom. I mean, goodness, Reed, there are plenty of other girls for you... there must be. Heaven knows there are plenty of other men."

"Jesus," Reed whispered. He stared at her, uncomprehending. She sounded like a stranger, a woman who had never heard of morals, or human decency. She was a stranger, an empty stranger, talking like this.

"Oh, Reed." She frowned. "Why did you come here? We just fight all the time. All the time. Why'd you have to follow me here just to fight?"

He spoke in a dull, dead tone. "You are my wife, Milly." He no longer even expected her to understand what this was supposed to mean. "You are my wife."

"Well, I don't want to be!"

"Milly." He sounded desperately tired, barely able to speak above that hoarse whisper, saying all the things to her now to her face that he had said aloud, alone in his car, speeding across unnamed, unchartered states, talking it out with her. "For God's sake, Milly. Haven't you any sense of morals?"

Her head tilted. "Don't start talking about my morals. My morals are just as good as anybody's morals. Harve and I are going to get married. Just as soon as we can."

Reed's young shoulders sagged in his wrinkled Orlon jacket. He stared at Milly, shaking his head. His voice had bitter wonder in it; he was completely defeated, without even comprehending what was beating him. He had never realized a person could come completely unequipped in the department which controlled remorse, responsibility, consideration for the feelings of others.

He winced. "You can't just — just change men, Milly, like you would girdles... take one off and put on another one.... We — took vows. Before God. You and I... for life."

She was tense, withdrawn from him. "You didn't tell me — or God — the way you were going to treat me, Reed." Her eyes glinted with tears. "I — I won't be married to you, any more. I won't go back — home — with you. I won't, Reed." Her mouth quivered, but her jaw set in a stubborn line. "I'd rather be dead."

"All right, damn it," his voice shook, "if that's the way you want it — "

"Now, wait. Now listen here, Hall." Duncan strode forward,

trying to keep his voice calm, trying to set a crust of cool reasoning and logic over their emotions. "This is a civilized society." He glanced around, suddenly doubting even this. "Well — among our kind of people, it is — "

"Don't do me any favors, Duncan." Reed pulled his gaze from Milly, but he hated even having to look at the older man. "Don't include me among your kind of people. I'm not. I believe in the sanctity of a man's home, and marriage vows, and human decency, all the things any square believes in — I'm not your kind of people. And if you want me to kill you faster, just keep handing me insults like that — "

Poole laughed suddenly and Reed jerked his gaze around, stopped talking abruptly. But Poole was only pleased that a man as young as Reed could knock the props from under a big shot like Duncan. He enjoyed things like that. Fletcher turned, relaxing slightly, and staring at Poole oddly.

But Duncan was not even aware of them. He knew he had to put across his tone of logic with Reed Hall.

"We are civilized at least," he said, compromising. "We're supposed to be."

Reed's mouth twisted. His eyes glinted. "What's civilized about what you've done? Is it supposed to be so damned smart and fashionable to walk off with another man's wife? Hell, men walked off with other men's wives from caves, you stupid clown."

Duncan exhaled heavily, but his voice remained level; he was a man who prided himself upon remaining outwardly calm in the wildest proxy fight. "I don't want to argue with you, Hall. You're convinced you have legitimate right to outrage. Well, perhaps, except that a woman is a human being. As much as you. With a right to make her own choice. She can choose for — "

"She did choose," Reed said coldly. "She chose me."

"I made a mistake!" Milly cried.

Carrdell had moved forward silently. He reached out, touched Reed's arm. Reed reacted, shaking all through his body.

"Give me the gun," Carrdell said to him in a flat tone. "You don't need to kill anybody yet... maybe the three of you can talk it out."

Reed shook his head, but Carrdell gently disengaged the gun

from Reed's fist. Reed's arms fell to his sides, and Carrdell stepped back, staring at the gun, but Fletcher, moving in lynx-like suddenness was upon him at once.

"I'll just hold that gun for you," Fletcher said. "You mind, Carrdell?"

Carrdell glanced at the gun, then at the cold smile pulled on Fletcher's death-mask face. He shrugged, handed the gun to Fletcher. The lean man dropped it into his jacket pocket and let the odd smile widen across his mouth.

He stared into Carrdell's face. "We don't want guns floating around loose, do we, Carrdell?" he said, taunting him.

Reed Hall was still trembling, but he seemed relieved to be free of the gun. He hated Duncan, wanted him dead. It seemed he could never rest again until he could look at Duncan's wax-dead face. But, why not face it — he wasn't a man who could kill anybody — unless he were to act in a violent rage — not even a man he considered as vile as he felt Duncan to be. The big man, taking anything he wanted, walking on anybody who got in his way.

"Now that we can talk reasonably — " Duncan began.

"We can't talk," Reed snarled at him. He leaned forward, ready to lunge at Duncan's throat. He seemed more a man, surer of himself, without the pawn-shop gun. His voice shook, his nails dug into his palms. "We got nothing to say to each other. You're a rotten dirty man chasing after young women, not giving a damn about their homes, or anything — just feeding your own lech, that's all."

Duncan did not retreat under the threat of Reed's violence. His face paled and he stood taller, his own hands clenched. His voice shook, whether he wanted it to or not.

"I assure you, Hall, that I am just as — "

Duncan gasped for breath, and jerked his head as if the room and everybody in it were spinning around him, wildly spinning. He stopped speaking. His face went ash gray, cheek muscles rigid, as if he were suddenly stricken with pain from his toes to the crown of his head. He bit down hard on his underlip, and dug viciously at his breastbone with his tensed fingertips.

"Harve!" Milly cried, heeling around. "Harve! What's the matter?"

Harvey remained poised, tall there for a moment, like a giant pine that had been chopped close to the ground but remains rigid for one last instant.

"Harve," Milly said. "What's the matter, Harve?"

Harvey breathed out heavily. "I — I am all right," he said.

"You're ill, Harve," Milly whispered. "Let me — help you to a chair."

"I'm all right." But Harvey's face pallor remained, and his eyes were stricken as if he had seen something terrible and frightening and did not see how he could look at it again. "I'm all right. It's just that — that breakfast we ate. All the grease, and hurrying. And now — all this."

Harvey looked around, pale. Milly tried to help him to a chair, but he pulled free of her. He backed away, leaned against the wall.

Reed stared at them a moment, then heeled around, strode across the room. His face was bleak when he stopped, and he spoke coldly and cruelly across his shoulder. He hated himself, too, because he could not understand how Milly could involve herself in anything like this, how that old man could let her. He hated both of them.

"There he is, Milly." Reed's voice was hard and flat. "There he is. Your *old* lover. Old. Your loverboy's an old man, Milly. You going to be his nursemaid, Milly? Is that what you want?"

Harvey remained leaning against the wall, breathless, but trying not to gasp for breath.

Milly looked at Harvey and then at Reed. Her face was taut with anger.

"Shut up, Reed," Milly said. "You don't know anything about it. That's what I'll be if that's what he wants."

"Christ." Reed's voice was low, full of contempt the healthfully young feel for their elders. "Can't even keep food on his stomach — and he's chasing a twenty-two-year-old dame. Jeez."

Harvey remained a moment longer, leaning against the wall. "Indigestion," he said in a low tone to Milly. "That's all."

"Well, no wonder," Milly said, glancing at Reed accusingly. "All this excitement and raging. No wonder."

Carrdell exhaled heavily. He moved his fascinated gaze from

Milly and Duncan to Reed, standing taut-wound with rage and agony, then to Earle Fletcher and young Poole. He saw that George was standing near Milly, and he stared at George, a faint grin on his mouth.

"Look at this, George," he said in a mild tone. "You George. The way you hate me. Look at the mess other folks get theirselves into. Be glad you got me."

The mongrel dog merely growled, showing his teeth, one side of his mouth pulling in a sneering manner.

Milly, standing close to Harvey, was staring at George. She shook her head, laughing. "Well. That's the cutest thing I ever saw. That dog. He talks back to you."

"He hates me," Carrdell said. "But I'm trying to convince him that's just because he doesn't know anybody else to hate."

Milly sank down beside George, smiling. "Come here, George. Will you talk to me?"

Smiling, she reached out her arm and George snarled, lashing at it. Milly screamed, and threw herself backwards away from George, striking on her hip, and sprawling on the floor.

"Down, George, damn you!" Carrdell's voice crackled in the room and George subsided. George's hairs were bristled, and he was showing his teeth.

Milly stayed where she was, mouth parted and eyes round, staring at George.

"Smart dog," Reed said softly from across the room.

"Why that dog is vicious." Duncan straightened from the wall, staring at the mongrel.

"Yeah. I reckon he's vicious, all right," Carrdell admitted.

"How can you keep a vicious animal like that?" Duncan said.

"Well, but George isn't really vicious. Not as long as you leave him alone," Carrdell said. He gave them a warm smile. "George is just a rugged individualist, that's all."

Duncan smiled faintly, despite himself.

Carrdell nodded. "You see, George and me had to get one thing settled right from the start up here. This ain't like a city or a village. Nobody can depend on nobody but himself. Minute a man — or animal, like George — depends on somebody else to take care of him, why that man — or animal — he's a goner. I had to teach George that — "

"You made him hate you," Milly whispered in awe.

Carrdell looked at the lovely girl sprawled on the floor. He shook his head. "No. At least, not intentional. But him hating me just grew natural from me teaching him to depend only on himself. Natural-like. You see, you get to loving somebody — why, that can be dangerous, too. You worry about the one you love — instead of worrying about yourself. That can be fatal, too, up here."

"How sad," Milly said. "He's such a pretty dog."

Susan spoke from across the couch. "Mister Carrdell... please. Won't you help me?"

Carrdell jerked his head around, astounded. "My lord. So much on my mind... forgive me, little lady. I'll get right back to your husband."

Two long strides brought Carrdell across the lobby and he passed Poole, going around the couch. He knelt beside the couch, took up a knife and began cutting away the blood-clotted shirt.

He stared at the exposed wound for some moments. He winced, but glanced at Susan with a smile. "Don't see any way but to cut in there a bit," he said to her. "Hate to. Less you cut on a man, the better. But — no other way to get in there to that slug."

She nodded. Carrdell laid the two knives and the wire on the straight chair beside him.

Susan knelt at his side, holding Matt's head in her arms. Matt was breathing heavily; his breathing was the loudest sound in the room.

Carrdell's big hands moved expertly, quickly, slicing in deft short strokes, making small, deep incisions across the open wound.

Susan closed her eyes, pressing Matt's head against her breasts, not even aware how tightly she was holding him.

Suddenly Matt's breathing stopped completely. The silence seemed to gush forward, concentrating upon Matt's rigid, inert body. For a moment Susan did not even realize what had happened, only that there was some terrible change in the deep silence. She went tense, jerking her head up away from Matt's sweated hair.

12

Susan cried out, stricken.

But Carrdell was already moving. He shoved Susan aside so roughly she toppled on the floor, bracing herself against her hand, watching him, wide-eyed.

With one huge hand, Carrdell worked at Matt's solar plexus as if it were a bellows. He turned, fleetingly, jerked his hand at Milly. She seemed to read his mind, moving in and covering Matt's open wound with clean, wadded cloths.

Then Carrdell knelt over Matt, forced his mouth wide open by pinching his cheeks between his teeth. He pressed his face against Matt's and breathed into Matt's mouth, at the same time working that big hand against Matt's diaphragm.

Susan stared, eyes distended. She pulled herself to her knees, and crouched there. Her eyes dilated, and she sagged against her heels, almost fainting. She reached out, caught the couch arm, dug her fingernails into it.

Milly leaned forward, fascinated, staring at Carrdell working over Matt. Duncan said something to her, but she didn't hear him. She made a downward gesture with her free hand but didn't turn her head.

Reed heard Duncan ordering Milly to stay back out of Carrdell's way. He scowled at the manner in which Duncan ordered her around, and at Milly's acting as if Duncan were part of her life— as though she and Reed Hall had never lived together, gone to bed together, stood before a minister together.

Poole turned, leaning against the couch back-rest. He rested his weight on the flat of his hands. He watched Carrdell a moment in grudging admiration, and then lost interest, and stared down at the top of Susan's rich black hair. He licked his mouth, talking to himself.

"Goddamn ... oh, ringadingdingding, leching damn ... god-damn ... money ... Oh, man. Hash. Dish, ringing, thringing, singing ding."

Earle Fletcher had not moved since George had slashed out at

Milly's hand.

He stood, apart from the others, not interested in the operation to save Matt Bishop's life, not touched by it, aloof. He had dealt in death by violence all his life. He had no interest in getting bullets *out* of men.

But he had found a sudden and terrible interest in George.

Fletcher bent forward slightly from the hips, staring down at the mongrel dog. His black eyes were deep set, piercing. He fixed his gaze on the dog's eyes, did not waver.

Slowly, as if troubled by a pesky deerfly, George turned his scarred muzzle upward and looked at Fletcher, malevolence showing in his flat, gray eyes.

"Hi, dog," Earle Fletcher said, voice soft and intense. "Tough. Huh? You a tough dog? Don't like nobody, huh? You and me. We ought to get along. Only, understand me, dog. I'm the boss. Had a dog like you once. When I was kid. Not big as you. But tougher. Lot tougher. Had to kill that dog when it wouldn't do what I told it. I'm the boss. No dog — nobody — gets along with Earle Fletcher that don't do what I tell him. You dig that, dog? Come here, dog. You know I can touch you, can't I, dog? You know what I'll do to you if you snap at me. Huh, dog? You want your teeth pulled out, one by one? Huh? Okay. You just snap at me, and I'll get pliers, and I'll take them teeth out. One by one. The hard way." He lowered his voice. "You know that, don't you, dog?"

As he spoke, he moved slowly forward, keeping his gaze fixed on the dog, his tone of contempt soft and yet almost chanting.

George stirred, flesh quivering. He continued to stare upward, confused now, and, under that voice, cowed for the first time in his life. He rose to his haunches, backed away one step, almost snarling, and yet not quite daring to snarl.

Fletcher grinned, in a cold flat way. "You got the message, dog? You know I ain't scared of you. Don't you, dog? So that means you got to be scared of me. Huh?"

He laughed in his throat, in contempt. "Nobody touch you... I'll have you whining with your tail between your legs... two days, dog... give me two days and you'll be too yellow to whine."

He laughed aloud suddenly, pleased with himself.

He reached out his hand, slowly, and yet without caution or any trace of fear. There was no aroma of fear for George's senses to react on. George's legs trembled, and his flesh quivered along his thighs.

Fletcher's hand came down slowly toward George's flat skull, slowly, fingers spread.

George crouched lower and growled, deep in his throat, hairs bristling along his scruff.

Fletcher's hand did not waver, came down on George's head, but abruptly the dog snarled, yelped and lunged away. George slithered across the room, growling, body so tense even its briar-pocked tail stood stiff. George crouched against the wall, lowered himself and stared at Fletcher across his paws. For the first time in his life George had faced an enemy unknown to him: fear.

Carrdell sat back on his haunches, panting. Matt was breathing again, in a labored, tired way.

Carrdell glanced at Susan. She was gouging the couch, face set. "You watch him close," Carrdell said to her. "If his breathing slows, gets weak, you help him breathe."

"How?" she whispered. "How?"

"You press your mouth hard over his and you breathe with him."

Susan's face was white, rigid. She nodded.

She pulled herself closer to Matt, thankful for one thing at least. She had to watch Matt's face. She could no longer stare at that knife in Carrdell's big fist, slicing and probing into Matt's side.

She closed her lips tight, staring at Matt's face. The sweat formed on her forehead, swelled into glistening marbles, ran down into her eyes. She did not move her head, or blink.

After a long time, she heard Carrdell exhale at her side, voice low. "It's out. I got that slug out."

But Susan was afraid to pull her gaze from Matt's face. He looked so gray. The gray of three-day ashes. The kind of gray you saw in a coffin at a funeral parlor, the kind not even the mortician could conceal. And his breathing frightened her — so odd, irregular, and so full of agony.

She glanced once to see what Carrdell was doing. He had opened the quart Mason jar. He was pouring the muddy, thick-looking liquid into the open wound.

Susan gasped, whispering. "My God. What are you doing?"

"Matt ain't out of danger yet, Miz Bishop."

"What's that stuff?"

"Indian herb remedy, m'am."

"It — looks filthy."

"But it ain't. You got to trust me, m'am. You trusted me this far."

She held her breath. She'd trusted him because there was nobody else to trust, nothing else to do. She'd stared at those thick fists, going wild with fear because how could fists so big be gentle and precise enough to cut vitally into a man without killing him? And yet, he had been gentle, easy, certain, even with the sweat in his eyes.

"Yes," she said. "All right."

She turned her head, looking again at Matt's face, her eyes brimmed with tears. Still, that stuff looked like gangrenous bile. Her mouth quivered. She heard Carrdell capping the ugly liquid in the jar again. It was so repulsive looking. Suppose that filth killed Matt when he might have lived after the bullet was finally removed? She bit down on her underlip to keep from protesting aloud.

She went on staring at Matt's face. The deep, agonized breathing slowly subsided, the sound of pain went out of it, and then, only moments later, it was as if he were breathing in sound, normal sleeping.

She turned, staring at Carrdell.

He smiled. "Something the Indians put in that stuff, m'am. Real soothing drug of some kind. It just plain takes the pain out of anything that ever hurt. Why, I've seen a raving mustang quiet down in minutes, start smiling, and eat right out of your hand."

He uncapped the whisky bottle, offered her a drink. Abstractedly, thinking about the Indian remedy and wanting to believe him and unable to, she shook her head.

Carrdell took a long deep pull at the whisky.

"That looks real good," Milly said, at his shoulder. "You mind if I join you?"

Carrdell turned, smiling and gracious. "Why, I'd be pleased for you to join me, m'am.... Though I better warn you. This here is a lightning juice that I distill for myself. I can't abide that sissy stuff they sell in the towns no more."

"I like good whisky," Milly said. She pressed the bottle against her mouth, punched her knotted fist between her breasts and took a long swig.

She jerked the bottle from her face, swinging all the way around, gasping and coughing.

Carrdell caught the bottle first, capped it, and set it carefully on the chair beside the knives. Then he caught Milly's flailing arms.

She was still gasping for breath.

"You all right, m'am?"

She coughed, exhaling. "Wow! Ringadingding. That stuff'll put hair on your chest, all right."

Carrdell smiled. "That's a horrible thought, right there."

They looked at each other, and then laughed.

13

Carrdell removed the knives, wires and blood-stained cloths, carrying them through the rear door toward the kitchen.

Susan pulled the straight chair close to the couch where she could watch Matt. She could not believe his suffering had been relieved so magically and that he had gone into deep sleep. She moved her eyes, studying his face: it looked smooth and young again, even if it was still gray, and his breathing was even.

Reed Hall came around the couch, picked up the bottle of shine.

Milly gave him a mild, condescending smile, but then she turned, staring with a faint frown through the rear door where Carrdell had gone.

Reed carried the bottle to the fireplace. He took a deep drink. He shuddered all the way through. For a moment he thought he would vomit; it was hotter than three spoons of tabasco sauce.

He leaned against the fieldstones, glanced at Milly. She wasn't looking at him, she was watching that rear door, but still he wouldn't give her the satisfaction of laughing at him because he couldn't hold this moonshine.

He gripped the bottle, and then saw that Duncan was watching him with an odd smile. Duncan was sitting at the old kitchen table now, braced against it, his own face pasty. The hell with you, Harvey J. Duncan.

Reed took another quick drink. This one sat easier, and he knew he had it made. He went over to the big chair, flopped into it with bottle in one hand, cork in the other. He'd found a friend in Lust, New Mexico.

Poole had not moved, but now he stood up behind the couch, licking his mouth. He moved his heated gaze over Susan one more time, then walked to where Fletcher was standing, half across the lobby from the mongrel, but still staring at it with twisted smile.

"He's scared of me, Poole."

"What?"

"The mutt. I can't stand a dog that ain't scared of me. Look at that mutt. He gets the runs just looking at me. Give me a little time, I'd have that mutt crawling on its belly."

"Yeah. Yeah." Poole glanced toward George, but wasn't interested. Sometimes this Fletcher was a real weirdo.

"Mutt wanted to bite me." Fletcher laughed. "He was scared to do it."

"Crazy. Reckon he's scared he'll get rabies. Huh?"

"Funny boy. You're funny."

"Fletch. Look. We got to get moving. We ain't got no time to fool around with mutts. That farmer hick has got the bullet out of Bishop. Why don't we get moving?" He glanced over his shoulder. "Tell Bishop's wife what she's got to do. Tell her why we're up here, and why we got her up here. We stalled long enough, Fletch. Too long."

Fletcher pulled his twisted, smiling face from George to Susan Bishop on the chair beside the sleeping Matt. He nodded, glancing once more at the dog. "Yeah," he said. "You're right. I'll talk to the chick."

Poole stared at Fletcher, frowning. No time for dames, but

worrying about a vicious dog. A real weirdy.

Fletcher picked up a straight chair from beside the old, slick-topped pine table. With elaborate carelessness, he carried it around the couch and sat at the end of it, over the rounded armrest above Matt's sweat-matted head.

"How's the boy?" he said to Susan.

Susan looked up, hardly recognizing Fletcher. After a moment, she nodded. "He's sleeping. I don't know how Mr. Carrdell did it, but he seemed to soothe Matt right off to sleep, as if the pain just stopped. Like magic."

"Yeah." Fletcher scarcely heard her. His mind was whirling ahead, thinking, clicking. "Yeah. Sure ... now, chick, you and me, we got to have us a little confab. Right?"

"What do you want with me?"

He did not smile. "Look. So let's save time. You was smart enough to know we got that map into Yucca City to you. You figured it out we wanted to see you. Alone. Now, let's keep it smart. You know by now, I would never of taken no chance sending word to you, but I got in a bind, and I figured maybe a smart chick like you could help me get out of it."

"What do you want me to do?"

"Well. It's kind of simple, really. We got no wish for the cops to get us, Poole and me. You can see that?"

"Yes."

"Me and Poole. We broke prison. Only jailhouse they ever got me in. I didn't like it. I don't mean to go back. Some other joes with Poole and me, all rounded up. But me and Poole outfoxed them Freemen, and we figure to keep on outfoxing the law. It would of been like a breeze, only like you know, that bank guard got heroic and plugged your husband."

He stared at her, black eyes cold with something in them that troubled her.

He laughed gutturally, as if at some secret joke. "So now we got a sick man on our hands. And to make it worse, we stopped Tuesday at some hick sawbones' place, thinking he could take the bullet out, and no questions asked, but this jerk stepped into the next room for his surgical kit and called the cops on us." His lean-fingered hands worked on the couch arm. "So, we carried Bishop between us and flaked out, just ahead of the cops. But they sewed us up in this area, pretty well. So far Poole and me managed to stay inside their roadblocks, and Poole was able to steal a car and get back into Yucca City Tuesday night to leave that map for you. Then we found this back road — and not much of a road — but it crosses an Indian reservation, misses any towns. We got up here, past here, and found out this road ends in a lot of places... But that's where you come in, doll. Like I say, we put our hands on a lot of geetus — three hundred grand, chick — and we got Matt Bishop. With a bullet hole in him. We drop him off and the cops get him alive, we're cooked. You dig that? We drop him off dead, fine, except that we're up here in nowheresville, with that money, but tied down. That's where you come in. Now. You hear me good. I figure a deal like this. Right down the middle. You help us. We help Matt all we can."

She exhaled as if she had not breathed all the time Fletcher talked in that low, tension-taut voice. "What can I do?"

"You can get that money across the Mexican border for us."

"Me?"

"You. That is if we can start you moving fast enough before the cops start looking for you."

"Maybe they already have."

"Maybe. But you better pray they ain't. It's the gamble we got to take. We'll hide that money inside the upholstery on each side of the back seat of your car. I'm expert upholstery man. I'll take off them panels, put 'em back in minutes. Nobody can see they been off."

"Suppose — I took that money to the police?" Susan was staring at Matt's face.

Fletcher shrugged. "You don't care what happens to your ever-loving there, okay. But I'll take that chance. We'll take care of your boy — you take care of our money. Real simple deal. If they stop you at the border, even if somebody recognizes you, even if they are sure you have gotten word where Poole and me have taken Matt Bishop — still they won't expect you to have that money with you. They won't look for it. If they look — they won't find it. All you got to do is get into Mexico: you wait for us in a burg called Villa Ahumada, and we'll show up in a few days — with your boy, Matt. And you got yourself an exchange."

She shivered. "What — will happen to Matt and me — after that? Won't the police know — something was wrong — your letting us go free?"

He shrugged. "Baby. Once I'm in Mexico, I don't care what nobody up stateside thinks. And you? Maybe nobody will ever really trust you and Bishop much no more — but you'll both be alive. You think about that."

"But — suppose they arrest me at the border?"

"Suppose they do? You don't know from nothing. And they won't be looking for money in your car. Sooner or later they got to let you go. Even if they send a tail to watch you in Mexico — once we're down there, it don't matter. I got it figured clean and neat, chick. Now, you can get your husband back, all nice and living — if he gets through this — and me and Poole get our money. Or — Poole and me — we take our chances, carrying that money with us — and you get nothing."

"You'd — kill Matt?"

He shrugged. "You get nothing."

She pressed her hand over her mouth.

"Make up your mind. What's to think, chick? I've already figured all the angles. Poole and me split up. When Matt can move, I'll bring him across the border. We can cross the border in a hundred places. Wetbacks do it all the time."

She straightened. "I — won't go — anywhere — without Matt. If you let me take Matt with me — I'll try to get your money across the border."

His mouth peeled away from his teeth. "Don't try to make deals, chick, when you got nothing to deal with. You better start talking sense. You take the money. We take Matt. That way everybody can trust everybody else. Now. You do it my way. Or we don't do it. You want Bishop dead? That's up to you. You can have that, too, if you want it."

14

Carrdell reappeared through the rear door carrying a large tray with a smoked and steaming coffee pot and several cracked cups, a Mason jar of milk and a package of sugar on it.

He smiled at them, beaming like the perfect host. "Got coffee for you folks."

He set the tray on the old kitchen table. He glanced at Susan who was white and rigid, unable to look at Fletcher, but unable to move away from him, either. "Better come have some coffee, Miz Bishop. You look peaked."

She exhaled, nodding. She got up without looking at Fletcher again, moved around the couch to the table. Why was she running away? She was glad to escape Fletcher even for a moment. But she was not going to make it. She was only running away from something she had to face, and could not face yet.

Fletcher stood up, face expressionless. He followed Susan to the table and poured himself a cup of black coffee, cradling it in both hands. He prowled slowly, taking long drags on the black coffee, looking Susan over, trying to read her, based upon what he knew about women, and the women he had known.

Duncan accepted a cup of coffee from Carrdell, thanked him with a curt nod, sipped it slowly. His face tightened with each sip as though the scalding fluid was burning its way across exposed nerves.

Milly filled a cup, added three spoons of sugar and poured in milk until the coffee was pale yellow in the cup. "Should watch my weight," she said to Carrdell.

He grinned at her. "I'll be pleased to watch it for you — m'am."

Milly giggled. Duncan's head jerked up, eyes bleak.

Reed remained in the dusty old club chair, staring into the cold dead ashes of the oversized fireplace. The moonshine he'd been nursing had given him a terrible clarity, and he was seeing symbolic things in the dead ashes. Only the shine anesthetized him and he no longer felt the sharp pain. He only looked up and shook his head when Carrdell offered him coffee. He sagged again into the chair, reading the ashes.

Carrdell looked at the people grouped about his steaming old coffee pot. He beamed his pleasure. "You folks enjoy this coffee while I rustle up some venison I just happen to have on hand. Some of the best meat you ever ate. Tender deer steaks from deers that have lived high up in these hills, so high damned few hunters ever climbed up there to chase them, so they never got tough and stringy from running in terror." He looked at them, smiling. "Tell you something else. There's no anger in this here meat. You know slaughtered meat has the stirred-up anger and fear in it — and that can't be good for you to eat."

Poole laughed. "What did you do, Pop? Tickle them deer to death with a feather?"

Carrdell glanced up, smiled. "Not quite. But I used a bow and arrow. Arrow in the heart. Quick. Almost painless. Never knew what hit him."

"Man, you're a marksman, huh, Pop?" Poole said.

Carrdell shrugged. He turned toward the rear door. Milly said, "Couldn't you use some help?"

He nodded, smiling. Milly set her cup down on the table and hurried out after him. Poole laughed in a sharp, abrupt way looking at Duncan.

Duncan placed his cup on the table. He noticed Reed turning his head and they found themselves looking at each other. Their gazes touched, clashed for an instant, then quickly dropped away.

Reed's face twisted with cold, laughing contempt. "Welcome to the club," he mumbled to the ashes in the fireplace.

Duncan did not speak but he could not restrain glancing toward that rear door, wincing at the bursts of laughter that rode through it. He sat there and massaged at his breastplate with his tensed fingertips — scrubbing, hardly aware he was doing it.

The deer steaks that Carrdell brought in on sizzling tin platters were thick and steaming. The aroma of them filled the lobby. Poole moved across to the table, fell into a chair and stabbed a steak with a fork. The others hesitated only a moment. Only Reed did not move from the dust-clogged club chair. He did not even smell the cooking meat.

They ate in silence, ravenously, washing down the food with coffee. For the moment they were thinking of nothing except the meal before them.

Carrdell brought out another pint bottle of white whisky. He offered it around. Susan shook her head. Duncan licked his lips, but involuntarily touched at his breastbone. He shook his head. Poole nodded, wanting a drink, but when he glanced at Fletcher, he changed his mind. "No," he said. "I can wait, huh, Fletch? Land of tequila, hot tamales and hot señoras. Huh?"

"I'll try it one more time," Milly said. "Maybe if I cut it. Three to one water."

She filled a tumbler with water from a metal pitcher, added a dash of white whisky and watched it ride downward like oil into the water.

"Here's to it." She took a drink and felt her face twist and rut. She replaced the glass on the table, ran to the fireplace, and spit out the whisky into the ashes. "This water! Why didn't somebody tell me? Tastes like rotten eggs. Whew! Worse than the whisky. Only that's hard to believe."

"Artesian," Cardell said.

"What?"

"Artesian well. You get used to the taste and smell — if you stay up here long enough."

"I doubt it."

Duncan got up, breathing deeply, some of the agony in his chest subsiding. He walked to the club chair where Reed sat and leaned against the couch arm-rest beside him.

Duncan took cigars from his coat pocket. He offered one to Hall.

Reed shook his head. He glanced up at Duncan, face cold, then returned his gaze to the fireplace.

Duncan flicked a lighter, held fire to a cigar. He thought about the agony that had almost blanked him out a few moments ago. He knew what anyone would say about his lighting a cigar now when only a minute ago he'd been suffering so badly he could barely speak. But cigars were a long habit, an old comfort, and you acted from habit, even when you knew better. And, he thought defiantly, he didn't care what a cigar did to him. He needed it. He needed something.

His voice sounded odd, weak in his own ears. "Can we talk, Hall?"

"I told you. We got nothing to say."

"Maybe we have."

"Sure. You tell me you're going to leave my wife alone. I'll say thanks. Big conversation."

"We can talk better than we can kill each other. No matter how much you hate me, Hall, murder isn't going to get you anything."

Reed's laugh was cold. "It won't buy you a hell of a lot, either."

Duncan shrugged. "I'm not afraid of dying."

"No? Anybody can say that. But you keep fooling around with my wife, and we'll see if you are or not."

Duncan exhaled, staring at the smoking end of his cigar. "Try to understand me a little, Reed."

"I don't give a damn about you."

"You ought to."

"Why?" Hall could barely bite off the word.

"Because you're full of rage now. You can hate me. You can see me as a man — old — who wants a young woman — at any price."

Reed glanced up. "Go look in any mirror, old man. See if you get any other reflection."

Duncan sighed. "I know what I am. A man who wants some good out of his life before it's too late ... that's all I am. I never meant to foul your home, Hall ... or steal your wife. But — even you should see that Milly doesn't love you any more."

Reed's hands turned white on the bottle, and he glanced up again. "How could she? You giving her minks, money — how could she love me any more?"

Duncan stood up, walked across the hearth to the fieldstone fireplace, turned, came back. "You know better than that, Hall. Inside you do. You've got to. You know that you have made Milly miserable for a long time. She — she didn't love you any more, she's stopped loving you — a long time before I came along."

"How the hell you know so much what happened before you 'came along?' "

"She's told me, Hall. Not once. Many times. You were — jealous. Unreasonable."

Reed's laugh was abrupt and bitter, and quickly dead. "Ho boy. That's ahead of you. Wait. Wait until she looks back at every guy in every bar she drags you into. Wait. You'll sweat around the neck, too, and feel helpless. You'll want to smash that simpering smile off her face."

"Would she do that — if she loved you?"

Reed stared across the hearth. "I don't know. But this I can tell you. She'll be doing it to you — most any day now."

He glanced across the couch to where Milly was helping Carrdell clear away the dishes, laughing at something he said to her.

Duncan turned, following Reed's gaze, watching Milly. He sighed heavily.

"Perhaps she will," he said.

"Perhaps."

"Still. That would be my problem. The fact is, she doesn't love you. Not at all. But you sit here and keep drinking, just keep tormenting yourself, and — you will kill somebody — and you'll go to the electric chair for murder. And that's all you'll get out of it."

"Don't fret yourself about me like this."

Duncan stared down at him. "I'm trying to make you see reason. Logic. Milly doesn't love you. She does love me. She wants to be free of you. She has made her free choice. And — don't think you can scare me, Hall, or threaten me. And don't think I'll ever give Milly up — unless she wants to be free of me — because I won't... Milly isn't a stick of furniture — chattel — that belongs to you. This is a free civilization, and she has made her free choice."

"Not once," Reed said under his breath. "Hundreds of times."

15

Milly carried out the last stack of soiled dishes to the kitchen. When she returned, Carrdell was wiping up the table.

"Now that we've had dinner," Milly said, glancing at the windows where the afternoon was graying, the silence deepening, "what do we do now?"

"Not a lot to do up here," Carrdell said.

"What do you do with yourself?"

Carrdell smiled. "Oh, evenings late like this, I sit out on the front stoop there and shoot at road runners and lizards. I seldom hit 'em. I just shoot at them."

Milly exhaled, looking around, frustrated. "How do you stand the excitement?"

She went around the old desk in the corner. On the shelf behind it was an old mahogany, battery-powered Zenith radio. She studied the knobs, snapped one on.

The radio whistled and crackled in the deep silence, and then a man was speaking, reading the news, " — and the chief of police in Yucca City has now reported that the wife of Matthew Bishop, bank clerk wounded during the daring daylight robbery of the Yucca City National Bank on Tuesday, has disappeared. Mrs. Bishop's car is in her garage at her home, and her mother, Mrs. Sybil Ames, hysterical when questioned by police, says she has no idea where her daughter might have gone. Mrs. Ames could not be questioned at length, since she was rushed to the Yucca City Memorial Hospital and put under sedation..."

Susan sat on the chair near Matt, staring at the old radio.

Fletcher strode around the couch. "Well, if that old biddy doesn't talk too much that'll give us a little time — "

"Police fear," the radio announcer continued, "that Matt Bishop, the young bank clerk taken from the bank at gunpoint as hostage — "

"Hostage!" Poole hooted from beyond the couch. "That's a great new word."

Susan jerked her head around, staring at Poole. He merely grinned at her, his eyes chewing away at her most nutritious parts, nursing. She moved her head away, shivering.

"Turn that thing off," Fletcher ordered.

Milly said, "But I — "

"You heard me, blondie." Fletcher took a long stride toward the old desk. "I don't talk to dames like you more'n just once. Turn it off."

Milly shrugged, snapped off the radio.

"Grouch," she said under her breath.

Carrdell said, "Here, George. Let's go."

The dog got up, snarling.

Carrdell moved toward the front door. George trotted after him.

Milly called, "Aren't you going to feed him?"

Carrdell paused in the doorway. He smiled. "Yeah. That's what I'm doing. Taking him out for a walk. He can run down a rabbit or something."

"Suppose he doesn't?" she said.

"He will. He knows. He don't catch something, he don't eat."

"But you've got all those scraps," Milly protested.

Carrdell shook his head. "Feeding George scraps would be the worst thing I could do for him. He'd get fat. Sluggish. When a sidewinder struck at him, he'd be too fat to get out of the way. Don't worry about George, m'am. Running. That's what keeps him lean."

Milly moved restlessly about the room, humming to herself. She snapped her fingers in rhythm to some remembered song. She looked the lobby over. "Dustiest place I ever was in." She giggled. "This Carrdell. He's even a worse housekeeper than I am." She lifted her head. "I'm glad you're rich, Harve... I'm the world's sloppiest housekeeper. You ask Reed."

Reed glanced up. "Don't ask me. You'll get no references from me." He took another long drink. He no longer even shuddered at the burn or taste.

Milly glanced longingly at the radio. "Some music would be nice."

"Sing to yourself," Fletcher said. He leaned against the tall old desk. He looked her over, mouth pulled down. "Light somewhere, bag. You make me nervous."

Milly paused, staring at him as if he were something new to her. "If I didn't love everybody," she said in an awed tone, "I could really work up a hate for you."

Fletcher stared at her, laughing in a flat way. "Listen, sister. It makes you feel good, you hate me. Hell, I used to drive dames like you — just like you — to a place in the country outside Manhattan." He laughed in that cold tone. "From there I don't know what happened to them dolls. I never saw 'em again. Never. Nobody in New York ever saw 'em again. Dames just like you. They used to hate me, too, them dames. It didn't change anything."

She turned her back on him, moving away. He looked her over, watching the automatic grinding of her full hips, unmoved by any faint flicker of desire.

He pulled his gaze back to Susan Bishop. He knew Milly Hall's kind, all right. But this Bishop chick was something else again. The respectable kick. PTA. Sometimes you didn't know exactly how to figure them.

He walked over, sat on the couch arm-rest, looking down at Susan.

"Baby, time is running out. I'm short on patience. Now let's quit stalling. I do what I can to keep this guy alive. But I'm getting tired of you. Like tired. You got no chips. You make no deals. You decide you don't want to move that money into Mexico for me — I quit fooling around." He leaned forward. "You got any idea how easy it would be for me to clamp my hand over this guy's nose and mouth until he just stopped breathing?"

He placed his big hand across Matt's mouth, pinching his nostrils closed.

Susan grabbed his wrist in both hands, jerking it away.

He laughed, staring down at her. They faced each other across Matt's prostrated body.

"All right." Her shoulders sagged. "I'll take your money down there."

He expressed no surprise, no enthusiasm. His voice remained business-like. "Okay. So let's get started. I'll stash the dough in the back panels of the Dodge, and you take off."

She shook her head. "No."

"For God's sake, chick." His eyes burned into hers, but he did not raise his voice. "Don't push me. Don't try to make deals with me."

"I — I'm not going until Matt — wakes up. If — he seems all right, then I'll go. You can get everything ready, but — "

"Don't crowd me. This guy may not come out of this for hours."

She shook her head, chin tilted. "I won't go. Not until I'm sure he's — got a chance."

He held her gaze. "He's got no chance at all, unless you do get going."

She twisted her hands in her lap. "All right. I need you but you need me too.... When Matt wakes up. When he knows me, and knows where he is — I'll go. I'll do just what you want — then." She swallowed hard. "That's no — deal, Mr. Fletcher. That's just — the way it is."

Fletcher leaned forward to speak to her again, his face a cold mask. But at that moment the front door was thrust open.

Fletcher lunged upward, turning, legs apart. His hand was already moving inside his jacket.

He exhaled heavily. It was only Carrdell with four or five blankets across his aims. Fletcher glanced at Susan, hating her. Damned dame. Now she had him jumping.

"It's one fine night," Carrdell said, the zest for living and the love of company in his voice. "Fine night. Hope you folks don't mind me prying around in your cars. I got a little cover here. There's old iron bedsteads and springs and mattresses in some of these rooms, upstairs and down, but I got no cover except one blanket of my own. All you folks had blankets in your cars, so I brought them in so you could be more comfortable tonight."

"Tonight?" Milly stared at Duncan. "Are you — are we going to spend the night here, Harve?"

Duncan shrugged. He glanced at the window, through which the darkness was like thick curtains. "It's dark now, Milly. We'd get lost out in those hills tonight."

"That's for certain," Carrdell said.

Duncan sighed. "I think we should stay until daybreak."

"Sure you should," Carrdell said. "Why, I just won't have it no other way."

But Milly shook her head again, shocked, her puritan senses outraged. "You mean — we're going to stay here — in the same hotel with — him?" She frowned, nodding toward Reed, chewing her lip on her concern for conventions.

"What else can we do?" Duncan inquired.

16

I'll just spend the night down here in the lobby." Fletcher said, looking at Susan. "I want to keep an eye on things."

Susan did not look up.

Carrdell placed the stack of blankets on the table. "That's a fine idea. How about you, Miz Bishop? Can help you fix a room?"

She shook her head, shivering. "No. I — I'll stay here near Matt."

Carrdell nodded. He placed old kerosene lamps along the desk top, lighted them, turned the wicks low. "All right. I'll bring in some logs and greasewood sticks. Might want a fire later on. It gets cold in here at night."

Susan sat rigid, listening to the wind rising, crying along the brink of the cliff, sighing in the streets, rattling boards out in the darkness. She shivered.

"Don't you worry about your husband, Miz Bishop," Carrdell said. "He'll be mighty comfortable on that old couch. That's where I usually sleep, right there, every night. He'll be just fine."

Milly took a blanket, folded it across her left arm. Then she chose a lamp, turned up the wick. "I might as well get some sleep." She glanced over her shoulder, accusingly. "Though I don't know how I'll sleep a wink with *him* here."

She paused at the foot of the stairs, staring at Reed. He finished taking a long pull at the bottle, glanced at her. "You slept under the same roof with me before, sugar. One more night won't kill you." He laughed coldly. "Maybe it won't. If you behave yourself."

"Oh, you're horrid," she said, helplessly. "Just horrid." She moved uncertainly up the stairs, holding the lamp before her.

"Take it easy on them steps," Carrdell warned her.

"And don't lean too heavy on them railings, either."

"My God," Milly said. She paused, halfway up the stairs. "Come on up here, Harve," she called. "I'm scared by myself. I've got goosebumps."

Duncan hesitated. He glanced at Reed, then he took a lamp

and blanket and followed her up the steps.

Reed stood up, his face rigid and white. He stared up at them, watching Milly pushing open the old doors, peering into the rooms.

He breathed out deeply and turned up the bottle, taking the last drink. He stood there a moment, as if about to fall when he no longer had the bottle to lean against. He walked slowly to the front door, opened it and hurled the bottle through it into the street. The sound of breaking glass was loud in the lowering silence.

He walked back across the room then and found the second bottle Carrdell had brought. He closed his fist on it. He glanced once more at the upper hallway, dark now. He shuddered visibly, went back to the club chair. He sank into it, staring into the cold hearth. He shivered all over, covering his head with his arms.

Carrdell brought logs and tossed them into the fireplace along with pine chips and greasewood sticks. He did not light it. After a moment he went across the lobby to the front door.

"Where you going, big shot?" Fletcher said.

Carrdell shrugged. "I better whistle George in, or he'll be around waking us all up."

Fletcher shrugged and Carrdell went through the door, closing it behind him.

Susan got up and took a blanket from the stack on the table. She returned to the couch and spread the dark cover over Matt. Poole leaned against the old registration desk, watching her.

Susan bent over to tuck the covers around Matt. Poole walked close behind her, pressing himself against her. He ran his hands down along her hips, the fabric whispering under his dry palms.

Susan lunged around, pulling away from him.

Poole laughed. "Come on, baby. Let's you and me go out and sit in one of them cars. Maybe the Caddy. That your style? You and me can talk. We got a lot to talk about."

He closed his hands on her arm. She writhed free. "Let me alone."

Fletcher turned from the window. "Let her alone, Poole. There'll be plenty of time for that."

"There's like time for it. Now. Right now." Poole was breathing fast. "There ain't no better time."

"Get in a room somewhere. And sleep." Fletcher's voice was sharp. "By yourself."

"Aw, Fletch — "

"Get going. Get some sleep. We got to keep watch. If I get tired, I'll wake you up."

Poole hesitated, considering. Then he glanced at Fletcher, at Susan, at Matt on the couch. He grinned, shrugged and nodded. He picked up a lamp, selected a blanket and sauntered slowly up the stairs.

Breathless still, Susan sank into the straight chair, watching Matt's face. She felt helpless, sitting there. There was nothing she could do to help, and help was needed so terribly, there was so much that needed to be done. Her mind whirled. There had to be some way she could get that money back to the bank in Yucca City, and still keep Matt alive. She knew better. What had Fletcher said to her? She had no chips. She could make no deals. She was helpless.

She shivered.

"Here."

She jerked her head up, hardly knowing who had spoken to her.

Reed was standing beside her. He pulled off his jacket, held it out to her. "Take my jacket."

"I — I'm all right. Thanks."

"Going to get cold," he said. "You'll freeze sitting there. Take my jacket."

"You'll be cold without it."

He shook his head. He held up the second bottle of Carrdell's whisky. "No. Not as long as this holds out."

He placed the coat around Susan's shoulders, and she looked up at him, smiling. He was not looking at her. He straightened, staring up the stairs to the shadowed upper balcony, the closed doors up there. His face was chilled, tormented. She wished there was something she could say to him, and knew there was nothing.

After a moment, he exhaled heavily, turned and walked back to the club chair. He sank into it, and stared at the dead ashes in the hearth.

Fletcher walked away from the window, prowling the room as if it were a cage.

He heard a whisper of sound, heeled around. It was George, padding in from the rear doorway.

"Hi, dog," Fletcher said. "Come here. Heel, dog."

George growled deep in his chest and made a wide path around Fletcher, going to the farthest corner, where he lay down against the wall.

Fletcher stood laughing to himself. Then he walked to the couch, stared down at Matt, checking him. The rages were building in him again. He turned, looking Reed over in the dust-streaked club chair. Reed was unaware of him. He took a long, solitary drink, gesturing at nothing with the bottle, gaze fixed on the fireplace.

Susan waited, but Fletcher did not speak to her. One moment he was there, standing across the couch, and then he was gone, moving on cat's paws he crossed the lobby, letting himself silently out of the front door.

Susan glanced up, startled that Fletcher was gone. She sighed heavily, stroked Matt's forehead, feeling herself shudder inside Reed's jacket. She felt the silence, thick as smog and damply oppressive inside this room, accentuated by the scream and whine of the night wind along the street and against the clapboard walls of the hotel. She felt chilled and frightened, filled with an unspeakable terror, afraid even of the density and the enveloping thickness of the silence. She looked at Reed, wanting to speak to him, to say anything that would break the awesome quiet. But Reed was oblivious of her.

Susan bit her lip, twisted, trying to get comfortable in the awkward, straight chair.

17

Susan came slowly awake, troubled, filled with a chilled sense of dread she couldn't even really understand. Her eyes opened, fearful, and for a moment she could not even remember at all where she was.

She moved her arm and a shaft of pain plunged through her. She was stretched awkwardly and uncomfortably on the straight chair. She felt blue with cold. She was shivering and her teeth chattered.

She sat up, tugging Reed's jacket closer about her. She tried to tell herself it was only because she was cold that she was frightened, but the nagging sense of wrong in the very atmosphere persisted.

The strange, eerie stillness in this place was almost like a dry mist; there was the suffocating sense of loneliness of the coffin. The night was a shroud closing down upon her.

She stared at Matt, willing him to open his eyes. She almost cried out his name, just to hear her own voice in the deep, still dark. A single lamp, wick turned low, glowed from the old desk. The corners of the room bulged with black shadows, and limber streaks of dark played through the light itself.

She heard the whispers of sounds, the sounds mice might make in a dry attic, and then a faint whispering of voices from the bulging shadows.

Outside the building she could hear the strong night wind, a sobbing sound, and she tried to tell herself the whispering she heard in the corners was a trick of the wind and the dry ancient clapboards. She was so cold. She glanced at the fireplace where Carrdell had left logs and kindling. Perhaps if she lit a fire she would feel better. And then suddenly the whispering sound struck at her back, and she sat up straighter, rigid, listening. Don't panic, she told herself, and felt the increase of panic, felt it building.

"Mister Hall ... Reed."

She whispered his name, her own voice no louder or any more familiar to her than the strange whispers from the darkness.

"Please... Mister Hall. Are you awake?"

In a kind of agony of terror, she saw he wasn't awake. If he were sleeping, it was the deep slumber induced by fatigue and frustration and white shine. He was slumped in the deep chair in shirt sleeves, as if he had passed out. Crocked. Finished.

Oh, God. She felt her teeth chattering. She spoke his name again, but without any hope in her voice at all. He looked so vulnerable, and hurt, and helpless, like a small boy crouched deep in the chair for some warmth. The second bottle was empty at his feet. Even with the little she knew about him, even through her own agony over Matt, and the new dread that half-paralyzed her, she felt sorry for him. He looked so alone, so lonely, so defeated. He was beaten, and he knew he was beaten, but he did not know how to surrender. And now he had nursed on a bottle until he was unconscious; he had finally found one temporary escape. Exhaustion and drinking had caught up with Reed Hall; the hours of driving steadily, unrelentingly, searching unblinking, the hot coffee in the strange roadside diners, and now the frustration and the whisky had knocked him out.

A board slapped somewhere. The wind. It had to be the wind.

A dry door scraped on a warped flooring, distantly. Some of the others, moving around in the dark.

The old stairs creaked, keening dry and loud in the still night.

She jerked her head around, slapping her hand over her mouth to keep from screaming.

The light from the desk cast only a wan saffron glow as far as the stairs. It was mostly in shadow, and the dark shadow there could be a man, or only a shadow.

There were steps from the hotel veranda and she pulled her gaze around.

A lean, spare shadow fell across the glass panes of the window, paused there. A man was standing out there, peering in through the window. In the darkness she could not recognize Earle Fletcher, but she was sure it was he.

There was nothing about the man to reassure her. But she felt a little better. He was out there, walking back and forth, trying to think his way out of this cul-de-sac.

She brought her gaze down and found Matt's eyes open. He

was watching her.

She almost cried out in her bursting sense of relief. There was a strange serenity in Matt's face; the pain was diminished in his eyes and he smiled faintly.

"Matt ... oh, Matt," Susan whispered.

"Did I wake you, Susie?"

"You? How? I don't think so. When I woke up, I thought you were asleep. Something woke me. Noises. This terrible place. I woke up cold. And afraid."

"I called your name. I was half-awake. I'm sorry I woke you, Susie."

She massaged her neck. "I'm not. I'm cramped and cold. And, oh, thank God, you're all right.... Are you in pain?"

He frowned. "No. I'm not. It's funny. I'm not in any pain. I feel warm all over, as if I'd been drugged, you know. And my side is numb, even when I touch it."

"Matt... let's get out of here."

"What?"

"Let's get out of here. You and me. Somehow. Let's get out of here."

An odd smile pulled at his mouth. "Susie, I couldn't even get up from here. I know I couldn't get up. I feel numb — I thought I was dead when I woke up — because the pain was gone."

Susie chewed at her lip. "What are we going to do, Matt?"

He supported himself for a moment on his elbows. "About what, Susie?"

"About those men ... those killers."

"Don't worry about them, Susie. You're all right.... For the first time since you married old Matt Bishop, you're all right."

"Matt, are you out of your head? What are you talking about?"

"I'm talking about us, Susie. You and me. No more living on peanuts in that hick town. No more dressing up like I got money so I can look slick and work in that bank, and owing everybody that will let me just so I can sport a clean shirt."

Her mouth sagged. "What are you talking about?"

"Us, Susie. You and me... and one-third of three hundred grand."

Her head moved back and forth. "Matt, you're crazy." Her

voice sang with tension.

"Am I? You think I wanted that drudgery we lived in for you, baby? No future in that bank? All that money I had to handle, and not see, and not think about, and not really touch? You couldn't glom on to a damned dime in that place. I've sat there and toted up three thousand bucks a minute, and didn't even have lunch money in my pocket. That's over. That's all over."

Her teeth chattered. "Matt ... please — "

"For you, baby. I told you I'd give you a mansion someday. And I'm going to. In South America somewhere. All the servants you want." He sank back and laughed mildly, staring upward past her. "Maybe I'll open up a bank of my own. But I guess not. I never would trust my tellers and clerks... . Don't you worry, baby. As soon as I can get on my feet, we'll get into Mexico, and — "

"Matt. You didn't — "

"I didn't what?"

"You didn't — help them steal this money!"

He nodded, voice low. "Oh, yes I did. I got sick of debts to my ears and my hair growing down over them because I could never even really afford a haircut... us wanting a baby we couldn't even afford, and a nice deep rut for me in that damned bank."

"Matt. Oh God, Matt."

Susan covered her ears with her palms, pressing hard, fingers spread and tensed. No wonder Poole had been making snide remarks about Matt all day. No wonder Poole told her she was no better than he was. She shivered, still numbed with shock, still too stunned to believe what had happened to her, shaking her head back and forth.

"Baby." Matt's voice was soothing. "Baby, it's going to be all right."

"Matt. How could you?"

"It was easy. It all happened so easy, like something that has been planned for years, maybe all my life. When I was a kid, I ran away from home, stole a car and got into some trouble. I would have spent time in a reformatory but a guy from out of nowhere came along and got me out of it, like greased easy. He was a lawyer. Later I realized he did a lot of work for big-shot hoods with loot. But me, I never saw him again. Forgot all about him. But — well, looks like he never did forget about me. Kept up with me. Knew where I lived. Where I worked. How much money I owed."

"Oh God, Matt — "

He breathed in deeply, didn't look at her any more. But his voice remained level. "So when Fletcher broke out of the pen, needed cash, and headed this way, why — this lawyer sent him to me. Told Fletch — "

"Fletch?"

"Told Fletcher I worked in this bank, needed dough, might be able to set up something for him — for a price."

She shook her head, staring at him.

"Don't look like that, baby. It was for you. And for me. Fletch and that Poole kid were hiding near Yucca City, and on Tuesday nights — when I was bowling — I'd drop by this cottage to see them, and we laid it all out."

Susan's mind clicked away, and she saw in her flashing memory the bowling bag near the front door waiting for him last Tuesday when he didn't come home, the way it was every Tuesday night when he went bowling. Oh God. She was still sleeping. Still dreaming. It was a nightmare, all this. It had to be.

"Matt, we — had everything. We had — each other — "

"We had nothing. But we're going to have. We'll get to Mexico, and then, bingo, baby, the whole, wide, wonderful world."

She was too ill to speak now. In bitter anguish she wondered if Mr. Carrdell had some magic Indian herb that would take away the emptiness and the pain inside her. Oh, it was beginning to hit her now, really hit her, and she shook her head, trying to deny her thoughts.

"Come on, Susie. We're together. In just a few days we'll be out of this. We'll be rich."

"No... I won't, Matt."

"You won't what, for God's sake?"

"I won't let you destroy us like this. We're — good and decent and respectable people, Matt... we've got to stay that way... it's all we've got."

"It's nothing. Nowhere. Less than nothing. I want money. For you. Both of us. I'm sick of poverty and all it'll buy you. Try to dig this, baby. I did this for you."

"No. Not for me. Don't say that."

"It's the truth. It's God's truth. I wanted to give you nice things."

"You gave me nice things, Matt. All the nice things I ever wanted — and now — you've killed us, you've killed us, Matt."

"Don't talk crazy like that, honey. Please."

"Matt. Listen to me. That man — Fletcher — wants me to take this money into Mexico in — mother's car."

"I know."

"You know?"

"I told him to send for you. When I got blasted."

She seemed to sag inside Reed's jacket. Her voice was dead. "You must have known me pretty well. I — told him I'd do it."

"That's my sugar — "

"That was — before, Matt. Before I knew what — what they had done to you."

"Done to me? That's for laughs, sugar. Nobody's done anything to me. Except that bank. Except that damned bank guard. You do what Fletcher tells you. He's a smart kook."

"He's a wild animal. That's all he is. That's what he'll make of you. Listen. I'll let him put that money in my car.... and I'll take it back to Yucca City — !"

"For hell's sake, Susie!"

She went on, breathless, "I'll tell them at the bank that I got it away from the crooks. That — they were holding you.... When I'm gone, you can sneak away. You can hide. I'll come back and get you... Poole and Fletcher won't know the truth about what I'm doing — and they won't ever know the truth back home — "

"Susie. You're talking like an idiot. You nuts? Fletcher would kill you if you crossed him. He'd kill both of us. We couldn't ever find a place dark enough to hide in." He caught her arms. "I'm sorry I've hurt you, Susie. I never meant to. I thought I was doing it — for us... but it doesn't matter... don't you see, whether we like it or not now, we're in it ... we got to go along with him, Susie. All the way. It's the only way we can stay alive... and, we'll be rich, Susie."

She pressed her hands against her face. He reached out, trying to comfort her. She drew away from him,

She looked up, wan, cold, and empty. "I do see, Matt. You thought — you were doing this for me. I know you love me. I do know that — "

"You're all I love, baby."

"But I don't want it. Not like this. And I feel all dead inside, I feel — like I never knew what you were — what you really were until now — and I'm all dead. I don't know if — if I could ever — want you again."

"Baby, don't talk like that."

"It's the truth, Matt. I'm all drawn up. All sick. I know — I know I'm going to help you get away — if I can.... But I tell you this, now.... I don't want to see you any more, Mart... I never want to see you again."

He tried to sit up. He winced with pain, but ignored it. "Baby, be human, baby. Try to understand the spot I'm in. The spot I been in... I love you, baby. Please."

He reached out, tried to pull her to him. She moved away, shaking her head, and loving him, and crying inside, her face a white, lying mask, all cold and empty and dead.

18

Susie heard footsteps on the stairs behind her. She wiped at her eyes with the back of her hand and turned slowly.

She caught her breath, staring.

Poole was coming down the creaking stairway. His thick, curly hair was awry. His eyes were puffed, swollen, sleepless. His undershirt bulged with the heavy cords of muscles across his chest. His slacks were wrinkled and he was barefooted.

He paused when he saw her recognize him. "Hi, baby. Where's all the people?" He laughed. "Never mind. I've got something for you, baby. Have I ever got something for you."

He sprang off the steps lightly, mouth pulled askew by his grinning.

Susie stood up, knocking over her chair.

"Why, don't be scared, little girl." Poole laughed. "It's like candy. I got like candy for you, little girl. Why, I ain't going to hurt you... you and me. We're gonna chat for a few minutes. Like talk over old times. Get to know each other. Maybe couple minutes that jazz, then we're gonna love — for a long, long time. I got a terrible need built up in me, and I got to tell you about it."

He licked his lips, panting across parted mouth.

"Man, oh ringadingding, you take the scales right off the walls, and that's like for a man gets a woman regular... Now you take me. I been in a cage for a long time — and I never did see anything like you, not in the hottest dream I ever had in that cage where I dreamed — reckon I forgot they even made 'em like you — "

"Matt."

Susan moved her head, seeing Reed unconscious in the chair, and Matt helpless on the couch. "Matt," she whispered.

Matt tried to sit up. He gasped, shaking his head to keep from passing out.

Poole's gaze was attracted by Matt's movement, but only briefly. "Oh. You awake, fella? Well, you just lie there and don't get that bullet hole in an uproar. This got nothing to do with you. I got a few things to say to the doll here."

Susan jerked her head around. "Mr. Hall. Reed!" But Reed did not stir in the chair. She cried out again, helplessly, without hope. "Reed!"

Reed did not move.

Poole laughed, strode toward Susie. He caught her arm and pulled her body up against his body.

Matt said something. He bit down on his underlip until blood spurted down his chin. He pushed himself up, swung his feet off the couch, coming upward, dizzy, so the room wheeled and spun about his head, and his legs trembled under him.

Poole glanced at him, laughed. "Told you to stay out of this, damn it."

Matt lunged for Poole, grabbing at him with both hands. Susie cried out and pulled herself free. Poole laughed at Matt and casually stepped aside.

Matt staggered past them, trying to catch his balance.

Matt wavered, staggering, trying to turn around. Poole waited until Matt faced him, and then he struck Matt with his fist, low in the padding Carrdell had packed over Matt's wound.

Matt gasped, gagging. He doubled up, slowly, in terrible slow motion, clutching at his stomach, head thrown back and gray with agony.

He sank to his knees in that same slow movement, and toppled out on his side. He sprawled on the floor, unconscious, and did not move.

Susie ran to him, but Poole snagged her around the waist, digging splayed fingers into the protuberant roundness of her stomach. He clapped his other hand over her mouth, pulling her head back against his chest.

As if she were a rag doll, Poole lifted Susie like this and carried her to the couch.

The front door scraped open along the floor, loud, thrust open roughly.

Fletcher stepped through it, collar turned up about his neck, coat buttoned.

"That's far enough, Tommy," Fletch said to Poole.

Poole jerked his head up, still holding Susie, her toes inches from the floor.

He stared at Fletcher, eyes distended. He shook his head, voice frantic. "Now you stay out of this, Fletch. Now. I done what you said. All the way. But this. I got to have me this. You ain't gonna stop me, Fletch. You ain't gonna stop me."

Fletcher closed the door, leaned against it, watching Susie struggling against Poole's hands, considering it.

His voice was level. "She's got to take that money across the border for us, kid."

Poole panted. "I ain't gonna kill her. She's had it before — what I'm gonna give her, she's had it before … I ain't gonna kill her."

"You foul her up, she'll cross us." There was no emotion in Fletcher's flat voice. "Is it worth a hundred grand to you, kid?"

Poole licked at his mouth, nodding. "Yeah. It is, Fletch. I got to have her. I laid up there in that room. I tried to sleep. I couldn't think about nothing else. It's been — a long time, Fletch. A long time."

Fletcher shrugged. His voice remained flat. "I tell you this, boy, I'm not going to stop you. It's nothing to me — as long as I get that money across that border. But you better know. You foul that up and I'm going to kill you."

Poole stood there a moment, holding Susie across him. He stared at Fletcher, standing across the room in the shadows. He saw the pen, and the cage, and the money, and a road into Mexico. He smelled the warmth and the fear and the cleanness of the woman in his hands, and he looked down at her and the way her body rubbed him when she struggled against him.

He looked up, panting, licking his mouth. "Just once then, Fletch. Just once. But I got to have her. Got to, God knows."

Fletcher shrugged.

Poole slipped his hand down from Susie's mouth, across her throat, clutching at the front of her dress.

She threw up her hands, clawing at his face. He struck her hard in the stomach. She gasped, and screamed,

Poole's hand ripped downward on her dress. She went on screaming, and he clapped his hand over her mouth and thrust her back on the couch. She kicked, clawed, but Poole laughed louder, prying her ankles apart, lunging down upon her.

19

Fletcher spoke from the dark shadows near the door, voice sharp: "Poole!"

But his warning was not quick enough to aid Poole, and not even the lynx-like Fletcher could react as swiftly as he needed to. He jerked at his buttoned coat, thrusting his hand inside it toward his holster, but before he could draw his gun or speak Poole's name again, Carrdell had entered the lobby from the rear doorway and was moving toward the couch.

Carrdell wore only Levi's, no shirt. He was barefooted. He had been asleep on the kitchen table beside the stove in the rear of the hotel.

Poole heard Fletcher's warning, but there was not time to react to it.

Carrdell caught him by the scruff of his neck as he lifted his head, lifting him as he might lift some kind of animal.

Carrdell brought Poole upward off the sobbing girl. Still holding Poole at arm's length, he let his feet scrape the floor, then spun him around and sent him stumbling back against the fireplace.

Poole struck hard, still too stunned to feel any pain. He caught his balance, bracing himself against the stones, staring at Carrdell as if he were something out of a bad dream.

Carrdell's voice was extremely mild. He glanced at Susie who had lunged upward, trembling, trying to pull her torn dress back across her body.

"This man troubling you, m'am?" he inquired.

Susan could only nod, still unable to speak.

Carrdell turned, regarding Poole. "You're a mighty impulsive fellow, boy. You ought to learn to ask a lady for goodies. And if she says no, why —"

He'd moved forward as he spoke, and suddenly he lashed out, driving the back of his hand across Poole's temple. Poole was crouched, but caught off guard, and he couldn't even lift his arm to shield his head. The sound of Carrdell's hand was sharp and loud against Poole's face, and the boy sagged at the knees, staggered and crumpled against the stones again before he could steady himself.

He straightened slowly, shaking his head, eyes distended, watching Carrdell warily. His nose was bleeding. He trembled, setting himself to spring upon Carrdell.

Carrdell stepped forward, like the left hand of God, but Earle Fletcher spoke coldly, moving toward them, "Hold it. Right there, Carrdell."

Carrdell paused, glanced over his shoulder, legs apart.

"The kid's got himself a hunger, Carrdell," Fletcher said in a cold, distant way from across the couch. "The kid's got himself a real seven-year hunger."

"Then let him buy his food somewhere else," Carrdell said.

"He's getting it here," Fletcher said.

Carrdell spoke in that level voice across his shoulder, still ignoring Fletcher's drawn gun. "You don't figure this little lady's got troubles enough?"

"It ain't your affair, Carrdell." Fletcher tilted the gun. "The boy wants something. This gun is buying it for him."

Poole was set now, and his head was clearing. He said, quavering. "Hold it, Fletch. I want this creep. Gimme that gun."

Fletch laughed in an indulgent way. He stepped forward a few paces, pulled Reed's, pawn-shop gun from his jacket pocket, tossed it underhand to Poole. Laughing suddenly, Poole caught it.

Carrdell was all over him before Poole could twist the gun around in his fist. He struck Poole in the left temple, ignoring the gun. The boy staggered, almost paralyzed.

Fletcher yelled. "Hold it, Carrdell. I'll put a bullet in you!"

He jerked the gun up. He heard movement beside him and pulled his head around in time to see a flash of movement from the shadows. George sprang upward from the corner, snarling, coming toward Fletcher, crouched like a wolf.

Involuntarily, Fletcher cried out, "Down!"

And for an instant, the big mongrel hesitated, shivering, growling deep in his throat.

Fletcher laughed, turned, and jerked his gun upward again.

In that flash of time, George lunged at his arm, a streak of gray fur, a blur of movement. George's opened mouth caught Fletcher's wrist, certain and true, dragging down on it as his fangs closed.

Fletcher sobbed out in pain. The gun flew from his hand. He jerked his arm upward, yelling, striking at the mongrel with his free arm.

George released the torn, bleeding wrist in that moment, recoiling. George landed on his feet, crouching again, trembling, looking more like a wolf than a dog.

The mongrel dog didn't move, but crouched there, gray eyes fixed on Fletcher, waiting for him to make a move toward his gun on the floor. George waited there, tense, between the man and the gun.

Fletcher took a half step, stopped. He caught his bleeding wrist in his hand.

Beside the fireplace, Poole tried to lift the gun again, fighting to thrust his finger in upon the trigger. But Carrdell struck him now in the right temple, and Poole could feel the sickness and paralysis moving down through his body, crumbling his nerves and muscle controls.

Poole toppled around on his heels, the gun slipping from his lifeless hands to the floor.

Poole staggered against the stones. They dug into his back, but he did not feel it. He stayed there a moment, then lowered his head, charging Carrdell.

He struck headfirst into Carrdell's bare midriff. Carrdell set himself, let the boy strike him and bounce off. He did not even breathe out heavily.

As Poole staggered back, Carrdell brought his fist upward into the boy's face. Poole straightened tall, and Carrdell hit him again so that Poole went out on his back. He sprawled on the floor, quivering, and covered his head with his arms.

Carrdell exhaled heavily then. He turned, looking around the lobby. Susie had sunk to the floor beside Matt, had cradled his head in her lap. Reed remained drunk and slumbering in the big chair. Fletcher was clutching his bleeding wrist, standing tall, unmoving, watching George. Milly and Duncan had come slowly all the way down the stairs.

20

Milly ran to Carrdell. "Are you all right?"

He nodded.

"You were wonderful," she said, awed. "I never saw anyone like you before."

Carrdell smiled. "How could you? You've never been up here before."

"No," Milly said. She glanced around the room, "No. That's too bad, isn't it?"

Something, perhaps the sound of Milly's voice mixed with his troubled dreams, woke Reed.

He sat up slowly, pushing his hands through his short-cropped hair, yawning, scraping his scalp. He stretched his arms. He whispered, still half asleep, "Milly?" He opened his eyes and looked around the dimly lit lobby. "Milly?"

Then he saw her, the coat thrown hastily over her gown, her blonde hair disheveled. His face twisted, and the bitter hurts flooded back into his eyes. He was awake now. He shivered, sorry he had spoken her name, betrayed his weakness.

Milly did not speak. She looked at Reed, frowning and troubled, and with something else in her eyes, too.

Reed stood up. He stared at Milly for a moment and let his gaze rake across her to Duncan at the steps. He slapped the back of his hand against his mouth, chewing at it, and moved across the lobby, jerked open the front door. The wind howled in through it before he could close it behind him.

Nobody said anything. After a moment, Carrdell turned up the wick in the lamp, glanced around.

"Cold in here," Carrdell said. "Why don't I make a fire?"

He removed wick and glass from a lamp, tossed kerosene on the pine kindling and greasewood sticks under the logs in the fireplace.

Milly moved forward, following him, watching him work. He scratched a wooden match across the stones, tossed it into the kindling. The blaze leaped upward, orange and purple and streaked with green. He stayed there a moment, watching it catch in the greasewood and lick at the logs.

"I never have," Milly said, in a low awed tone.

He glanced over his shoulder at her. "What?"

"Met anyone like you," she said. "I never have."

Fletcher pulled a handkerchief from his pocket and wrapped it around his fang-cut wrist. He took a step toward the fireplace. George snarled, crouching lower, as if ready to catapult upon him. Fletcher stopped. His voice was cold with the rages in him.

"I've seen your kind before, Carrdell. Your kind." He jerked his head toward Poole, still hunkered against the old desk, on the floor, nose and mouth bleeding, trying to shake the cobwebs out of his brain. "Tough. Tough with young punks. Big with talk. I've met your kind before, Carrdell. And I'm still in business."

Carrdell straightened, glanced over his shoulder, watching Fletcher. He shrugged.

Fletcher took another step and again George snarled. Fletcher turned his rage upon the dog. His voice was low, taut.

"Yeah, mongrel. You're good as dead. You hear that, you damned mongrel? Dead. Good as dead."

Duncan spoke, voice hard. "That's a gallant dog, Fletcher. Even you — a man like you — should appreciate that."

"I'll buy him an extra-fine tombstone," Fletcher said, staring at Duncan. "Like pure marble."

The fire caught, glowing and leaping suddenly when the greasewood ignited, the flames chewing ridges into the logs. Carrdell moved away from the hearth and gathered up the gun he had knocked out of Poole's hands. Carelessly, he thrust the gun into his hip pocket.

He knelt beside Susan and Matt Bishop then. Susan was crying softly, but insistently, unable to stop.

Carrdell said, "He'll be all right, m'am. I swear it."

"Yes." She sniffled, her head tilting. "Sure."

Gently, Carrdell hefted Matt's hundred and ninety pounds, coming up from his knees with ease. He laid Matt down on the couch, pulled the cover over him.

The front door whined, scraping open. Reed came through it and closed it behind him. He looked pale and ill. He was shivering in his shirt sleeves, and he hurried across the room to the fireplace. He stepped on the hearth, getting as near the fire as he could, thrusting his hands over the growing flames to warm them.

Carrdell straightened up. "Why don't we all go back to bed? Try to get some sleep." He touched Susan's shoulder, turning her toward him. She had stopped crying now. "I got a pallet made on the kitchen table, and the stove's burning in there. You're beat. Go get some rest. I'll sit here with Matt."

"I'm too ill to sleep, too worried."

"I'll watch him." He smiled. "I'll watch everything."

At last, feeling the fatigue and anxiety, the shock at what Matt had told her like paralyzing poison in her veins, Susan agreed. She nodded, went slowly through the rear door toward the kitchen.

Duncan checked the watch on his wrist. "Won't be long now before daybreak," he said. "Couple hours at the most." He glanced around the lobby, at Fletcher, at Poole, now getting up from the floor but bracing himself against the old desk. Then his gaze touched Reed, warming himself at the fire. "I've had it. I've had it here. I'll take my chances getting back down to highway 85. Get your things together, Milly. We're leaving."

"It's so dark," Milly said, not even knowing why she protested. She'd been the one so anxious to leave, and now she was not anxious at all, "It's not long to daylight. Let's wait, Harve."

Reed moved back from the fireplace. He walked around the couch and picked up the gun a few feet from Fletcher. George didn't even glance toward him.

"You go ahead, Duncan," he said. "You go on, leave, if you want to. But you're not taking Milly."

Duncan just looked at him. There was nothing but a faint flaring of an old contempt in his face.

He ignored the gun in Reed's hands with the same disregard that he displayed toward Reed's ultimatum. He turned, went up the stairs, not hurrying. He came down almost at once, carrying Milly's suitcase. "Come on, Milly. We're getting out of here. Now."

She looked around, emptily, "Harve," she protested.

Reed moved slowly toward the doorway, blocking it, gun held at his side.

Duncan did not even look at him. He was staring at Milly. "Let's go, Milly. While we can."

"Oh, Harve —"

"Look, Milly. For God's sake. Two of these men are wanted for murder, jailbreak, robbery. At this moment they are unarmed. Now, let's get out of here while we can."

Milly's shoulders slumped, but she did not protest again.

Carrdell said, "There's a water pump in the kitchen, Duncan. You can fill your radiator. Unless there's a break in your hose, you'll be okay until you can hit a town."

"Thanks, Carrdell," Duncan said. "You've been — a most extraordinary host."

"That's the truth," Milly said, still looking at him.

"Pleased to have you folks," Carrdell said. "Me. I admire folks like you — and Milly here. I've not seen a woman as lovely as her since there used to be dancing girls here in this old hotel when

I was a kid."

"Why thank you," Milly said, still staring at him. "I never did see anybody like you. Anywhere."

"Let's go, Milly," Duncan said.

Milly gave Carrdell a tentative smile, nodded. She moved slowly, unwillingly, following Duncan toward the front door.

Reed's voice was sharp in the stillness. "I told you, Duncan. You can go. Alone. You're not taking her."

Duncan paused a few feet in front of Reed, still ignoring the gun. "I've been threatened before, Hall. You better know. I'm a man takes what he wants, and — from better men than you."

"Maybe." Reed's voice shook. "But maybe they never felt robbed, or outraged."

Duncan shrugged. "Go ahead and shoot then, Hall. I'm tired talking about it. But I tell you this. I've no fear you'll ever press that trigger. I never did. You couldn't kill anybody."

"Couldn't I?" Reed's voice shook with rage, the hatred he felt against himself because he was afraid what Duncan said was true. He stepped toward Duncan, hating him, thinking of all the ways he hated him, all the reasons he had for hating him, quivering with hatred and bringing that gun up.

Duncan remained unmoved, watching him.

Reed's hand shook. The gun trembled in his fist. He stared at Duncan and then recoiled, horror in his face. A sob broke across his mouth. He stared down at the gun in his hand, repulsed. He shook his head, opened his fingers and let the gun slip from his fist.

"Oh God," he whispered, "oh God."

He sobbed again, covering his face with splayed fingers. He dug at his face, weeping. He sank to his knees.

"I'm not even a man any more," he whispered. He looked up, face stricken. "Oh God, Milly. This is what you've — done to me."

His head sank again, and his sobs wracked him, and he knelt there almost as if in agonized prayer. Everybody was staring at him.

Fletcher heeled around, swifter than a feeding cat. He pounced on the gun, scooping it up.

His face was gray. He raked his gaze across them. "Any you people think *I* won't use this gun? Any of you?"

Nobody moved, except Poole. He straightened and wiped the back of his hand across his bloodied mouth, laughing in a rage of laughter.

Earle Fletcher nodded toward Harvey Duncan. "You might as well put down that suitcase, big shot. Nobody's going nowhere. Nobody's going to tell no cops where I am. So just sit down and make yourself comfortable." He laughed, pleased. "Earle Fletcher just took over again."

21

Fletcher glanced toward the crouched dog. A smile pulled at his mouth. He said, "Poole."

"Yeah, Fletch?"

"Poole, Nature Boy there." Fletcher nodded toward Carrdell.

"Yeah, Fletch?" Poole wiped at his bloodied mouth.

"Nature Boy has a gun in his pocket, Poole, He don't need that gun."

Poole laughed. "He don't need that gun at all." He moved warily behind Carrdell, but remained watchful. He tugged the gun from the hip pocket of Carrdell's Levi's. Fletcher nodded, his grin deepening. "Earle Fletcher. Down once in a while. He don't stay down. Not long." He jerked his head toward the rear of the hotel. "Okay, Poole, bring that Bishop chick back in here. Time we got this show on the road."

"Sure, Fletch."

Poole pushed the gun under his belt and went through the rear door and along the back corridor. Fletcher leaned against the couch back, watching the other people, studying each of them, separately, slowly. All the people in the room seemed to be holding their breath; the silence swelled out of the bulging shadows.

Abruptly they heard Susan scream from the hotel kitchen. Each of them reacted, going tense, standing up. Fletcher's grin pulled wider, and he shook his head at them. The sound of Poole's hand across Susan's face was almost as loud as her scream, and somehow more painful. Milly winced, and sank against Duncan.

Carrdell straightened, turning slightly.

Fletcher's mocking voice stopped him.

"Take it easy, man. You been a hero. Already. That's where we came in. Relax, man. You got your bullet ordered, already."

Carrdell exhaled heavily. For the first time there were lines pulled about his mouth, and the pleasure had gone out of his eyes.

Susan came through the rear door into the lobby. She was pressing the backs of her fingers against her cheek, livid where Poole had struck her.

"Here it is, Fletch," Poole said.

Fletcher's grin remained flat. "You're a good boy, Poole. Earle's going to buy you some Mexican dolls. All you want."

"Sure, Fletch." But Poole stopped smiling. He dragged his hand across the coagulated blood on his mouth. "Sure." He stared at Carrdell. "But it's all right now, Fletch. There's something else I want." His gaze raked over Carrdell, "One hell of a lot more."

Fletcher nodded. "You can have that, too, kid." Poole nodded, staring at Carrdell, touching at his bloodied face again.

Fletcher spoke to Susan. "Time to go. I'll get your car all ready, girl. You're taking off for Mexico." He grinned and stared at the others. "You're lucky, chick. *You're* going somewhere."

Milly sucked in her breath, making an almost inaudible whimpering. Duncan touched her shoulder.

Fletcher moved his gaze to Poole. "Take over, kid. Don't shoot none of these good people — unless you have to."

Poole laughed immoderately at this. He held the gun loosely, watching them. Fletcher went to the front door. Poole backed toward the glass-paned window. "Keep you folks where I can see you," he said. He glanced at Reed, still crouched on the floor. "Get up. Get over there with the rest of them."

Reed glanced up. His face was gray, drawn. He stared at Poole for a moment as if he didn't even recognize him at all. Poole cursed at him, and finally Reed nodded and stood up. He walked woodenly, sank to the lip of the hearth. He did not look at the other people in the room, but stared fixedly into the fire.

Earle Fletcher pulled open the front door, stepped through and closed it behind him. Poole backed up, leaning against the wall nearer the glassed window.

A moment later the sound of a grinding engine filled the hotel. And after a few moments, another engine ground, but did not catch. There was a silence, and then the grinding started again in the last car. This car did not start.

The people in the room stared at each other. Troubled, Poole licked at his lips, pressed his head against the glass pane, attempting to see out into the night.

The front door was thrust open.

Fletcher charged in, raging. His fist was white on his gun.

He took long strides, gaze fixed on Carrdell, and stopped only inches from him, between couch and fireplace. The fire crackled on the logs and, except for Fletcher's rasping breathing, was the loudest sound in the still night.

"All right, Carrdell." Fletcher's voice trembled. "What's the gimmick? There ain't a distributor cap on any of them cars out there."

Carrdell shrugged. "I took them off."

"Sure you did, man. But why?"

"Why, that's easy. You folks are the first company I've had in a long spell. I wanted you folks to stay around here with me for a while. I reckon it was a selfish thing to do. But I do dote on company. Something fierce. I'm a man loves to have folks around him."

"We'll put that on your grave marker," Fletcher said, forcing himself to match Carrdell's casual tone. "So now you can turn over those distributor caps to me, or you've had it."

"Seems to me you already promised my carcass to the j.d, over there." He nodded toward Poole.

"Quit stalling. I'm not fooling, man. Don't push me."

Carrdell shrugged. "Go ahead. You can kill me. Sure." But if you do, you're never going to find those distributor caps... not one of them."

Fletcher took a step forward. "I'm tired fooling."

Carrdell grinned at him, an empty grin. "So am I."

"Come on, Carrdell. I can make you wish you was dead."

"I had a wife affected me that same way," Carrdell said. "She didn't get what she wanted, either."

With lightning speed, Fletcher struck Carrdell across the face with the fiat of the black gun. Carrdell took a step back, flesh torn across his cheek.

He stared at Fletcher. Now he was waiting for him to move again, but Fletcher read this, held steady.

Carrdell touched at the blood leaking from his cheek. "Okay, Fletcher. I reckon this is it. I like company, but I'm real sick of you, and Poole. More than a little sick."

"The distributor caps, tough man."

"Sure. I'm ready for you and Poole to go."

"The distributor caps."

"Only, I got to make a deal."

Fletcher laughed. "Sure. If you think I'll keep any deal I make with you. Say it."

"You'll keep this one. Because that's the only way you ever get any of those cars started. Only way you get out of here."

"I'm listening."

"I'll sell you your distributor caps, Fletcher."

"Yeah? So okay. I pay you and take it back."

"No. You pay me. I put away my loot. Then I deliver you the caps. That's the deal."

Fletcher could barely restrain his laughter. "Okay. How much?"

"The full amount of money you took from Yucca City bank."

Fletcher stared at him a moment, cold, and then he laughed. The sound burst from him. Carrdell shrugged, then he laughed, too. The others stared at them as their laughter grew, louder and louder, louder than the night wind, crazier, striking against each other's laughter, bouncing off the walls, like two sane men gone wild with the crazy idea that each of them had gone just as far as he could go. Neither was going to back down, and so all there was left was the wild sound of laughter, rocking them.

22

The cry of the night wind died down just before dawn. The logs in the fireplace crackled, and the stillness inside the old hotel was no longer so intense.

Fletcher sat near the glassed front window, face set, eyes shadowy with the rages swirling in his brain. He stared at Carrdell and knew that sooner or later he would come up with the answer, the key that would open that prospector up like an old door. He could kill him; he wanted to kill him; and Poole, sitting near him with a gun on his lap, was ready and anxious to kill him. But without the distributor caps, none of the cars out there would start, and only hell knew where Carrdell had hidden them. There were tortures that would make a babbling brook out of Carrdell, but Carrdell was tricky — if you got too close to him, pushed him too hard, you might have to kill him, and you didn't pick up the tricks like that in this game. He had to keep Carrdell alive until he got the distributor caps.

"What time is it?" Poole's voice was low, almost a whisper.

Fletcher checked his wrist watch. Two hours had passed since he'd struck Carrdell across the face with his gun. Two hours. He'd given Carrdell time, but time was going to run out. If anything went wrong — if the law closed in — getting out of here in a car wouldn't matter any more, and Carrdell had had it.

Fletcher stared across the dimly lit lobby, wondering if Carrdell had sense enough to realize that. He couldn't go on pushing Earle Fletcher too far, either. Nobody could.

"Almost daybreak, Fletch," Poole said. "We ought to get moving."

"I'll tell you." Fletcher spoke between clenched teeth.

"Let's work on that farmer, Fletch. We can work on him."

"Sure. And he makes one of us kill him — what we got then?"

"We got to get out of here, Fletch."

Fletcher exhaled heavily and did not look at the boy again.

He looked at the people in the room. If there were one of them that Carrdell cared anything about, he could work that person over until Carrdell came through. But Carrdell was like that mongrel dog; he cared for nobody.

His fist tightened on his gun. Okay, time was going to run out, even for that smart boy over there.

Duncan had sprawled in the club chair before the fire and fallen asleep, suitcase beside his leg. There was a boy never gave up. He still thought he was going somewhere.

Susan Bishop had lain down on the old couch beside her husband, her head at the other end of it. Fatigue and the warmth from the fire after the long cold night had overcome her, and she slept fitfully, whimpering in her sleep.

Reed Hall was sitting on the edge of the wide hearth, staring into the fire, unaware of what was going on around him. He was wrapped inside a ball of agony in his own brain — it was four o'clock in the morning, and there was no longer any whisky to sustain him, nothing except the blaze and warmth of the fire, leaping green and orange and gray up the chimney. Inside his mind he whirled on the same empty thought: the truth about himself, the terrible knowledge that Milly's infidelity had robbed him of his manhood. She had left him nothing more than a glob on these stones; he could not kill for what belonged to him, he couldn't hold a woman, he could no longer even feel any desire for a woman. He wasn't a man at all any more.

He heard Milly's faint laughter, but he no longer reacted to it. It didn't touch him any more, and he didn't look up.

Milly was sitting near the far end of the couch, only faintly reached by the fire from the hearth, but she was wide awake, staring up at Carrdell.

Carrdell had stepped into his scuffled boots and pulled on a corduroy shirt, but had not stuffed the tails into his Levi's.

He leaned against the old desk, looking at Milly as if it had been a long time since he'd seen anything like her.

" — I should have been glad to go," Milly was saying, with faint tone of awe in her voice, unable to understand why she had not been anxious to get out of this place. "I mean. When Harve wanted me to leave here with him, I sure should have been happy to go, all right."

"Yes."

She looked up quickly. "I mean, it was our chance to get away, all right. I mean, those men didn't have their guns, and Harve and I could have gotten away — "

"Yes."

She sighed. "And I should have been glad to go. At least there's a heater in that Caddy, and I never was so cold as I was up in that room where I tried to sleep."

"They're pretty drafty, those rooms up there."

"I couldn't even find a room that didn't have at least one broken window. The wind was like ice water. I mean, I never slept a wink — even before all the trouble down here. I was alone — and so cold — I've never been so cold."

Carrdell's brow tilted. "Alone?"

Her head tilted, and those wide eyes fixed on him. "Oh, yes. I tried to sleep in a room all by myself, but I never could stand sleeping alone in a bed. Since I was — thirteen. I need somebody in bed with me, you know? But — well, tonight, here and all, it just didn't seem proper. You know? I mean, sleeping in the same room with Harve and my own husband being right here in this hotel. It just didn't seem proper."

Carrdell smiled faintly. "We all got our problems.... You mind if I tell you something?"

"Oh, no."

"I'm pleased you didn't go... I tell you. I'm going to miss you — maybe I won't miss these other folks — but I'm going to miss you when you go."

Milly smiled, flattered, and chewed at her lip. "Well, thanks. That's real sweet. And — well, when I think about it, I guess the reason I didn't want to go right away was — "

"Me?"

"Like I said, I never saw anybody like you before. And it seemed so exciting here, the way you took over, and all — I was afraid I'd miss something. I know now.... Harve and I should have gotten away when we could. But it's been — exciting."

He exhaled, looking her over. "You think this is exciting. You should have been up here in this town when things really were exciting — it was a long time before you were born — and I was just a little tad. But there was excitement. Dance hall girls. Bright with paint, I remember, and red garters. I never will forget them red garters. They had mines up here then, and money —"

"Too bad it's all gone."

He licked his mouth, glanced at the others, lowered his voice. "What you mean, all gone? Wish I had time. I mean if you were here — I could show you what I've located."

"You? A mine?"

He whispered it. "Uranium."

"Uranium?" The word burst from her mouth, and she covered her lips with her fingers.

"Right."

"Oh, show me. Please show me."

"Honey, I'd like to. But we'd cause trouble trying to walk out of here."

"I want to see it. I never saw uranium."

He glanced at Reed, then at Duncan, sleeping; then at the two men watching from the shadows near the front door.

"Reckon it can't hurt anything." He straightened and Fletcher was instantly on his feet, gun ready. Carrdell grinned at him across the lobby. "Relax, man. Use that gun on me, and you'll be trapped in these hills till the cops pick you up."

"Smart boy."

"Sit down," Carrdell said, smiling. "Relax. When you're ready to pay for the distributor caps, they're yours. Wheel and deal, man."

"What you think you're doing?"

Fletcher came forward again as Carrdell got a lantern from behind the desk, struck a match to light it. He got a Geiger counter from a rear shelf and came back around the desk.

He appeared hurt that Fletcher was watching him narrowly.

"Relax," Carrdell said. "I'm not going anywhere."

"That's right," Fletcher agreed.

"Just going to show Miz Hall around." He glanced at Milly. "We'll be right back."

Carrdell kicked the Indian rug into a bundle near the couch. Now Fletcher and Poole both moved forward.

"I'm only Mrs. Hall temporarily," Milly said, watching Carrdell kneel and pull up a trap door in the flooring where the rug had been. "Why don't you call me Milly?"

Carrdell glanced up, ignoring Fletcher and Poole, who stood across the couch, watching him. Poole brought his gun up, but Fletcher laid his hand on the boy's arm.

"Milly," Carrdell said. "That's a fine name for a girl like you. Just like you. Fits. Got excitement in it." He stepped into the trap doorway and reached out his hand for her. "Watch these old steps, Milly. They're kind of shaky."

She leaned over, troubled, but took his hand and followed him down the steps. "Why, it's a hole in the ground."

"It's a tunnel," Carrdell told her. He helped her off the ladder to the ground, climbed up again. Fletcher and Poole were standing over the trap door. Carrdell caught the door from the inside. He grinned up at the two men and pulled the trap door closed over his head.

23

For some moments Carrdell led Milly in silence along the tunnel. She followed close behind him, her fist gripping his shirttail.

The light was not reassuring to her. It showed her other tunnels, and sudden darting shadows against deeper shadows, and dry webs, gray and thick. She shuddered, but moved forward with him.

Carrdell stepped out into an underground room twelve feet across. He snapped a switch on the Geiger counter. The sudden excited clicking of the machine was loud, vibrating all through the tunnel.

"Uranium?" Milly said. "Making that noise?"

"Place is full of it."

"Why you could be rich. The way it clicks. It sure sounds rich."

Carrdell nodded.

He turned and looked at her, his sun-strained eyes eating into the lush blue of hers. "Yes, I could be rich."

She stared at him, smiling uncertainly.

"Only I never cared about that before," he said.

"What?"

"No. What would being rich get me?"

"Why, you must be crazy! Why everybody wants to be rich."

"I never did. Never. Not till right now."

She swallowed, realizing suddenly that he was not talking about the uranium, or mining, or riches, and hadn't been all along. He was talking about her.

"Do — do you care about it now?" she said.

He nodded, staring into her face. "Now I care. A man needs somebody to work for. I haven't had that. I know how your husband feels — the young one, I mean. It would be hell to lose you. It must be hell for him."

"Reed should find himself some nice girl. He's real sweet. But — he's just not what I want."

"Maybe — he could be."

"No."

"If you just made up your mind that he was just as good as the next man that would come along, maybe better, then he could be."

"But I couldn't do that," she said

"You ever tried?"

"I've tried," she said, sighing.

"You know you can always find a man that looks good, if that's what you're looking for. Or the man you got can look good — if you let him."

"Poor Reed," she said.

"Too bad you can't go on back home with him. Huh?"

Milly bit her lip. Until a moment ago he'd looked as if he wanted her for himself. Now all he could talk about was Reed. Her voice hardened. "Sure. That would just solve everything, wouldn't it?"

"Wouldn't it?" He was still watching her face.

"No. Because I've been back home with Reed. I've been with him for a long time — it just don't solve anything."

"No. I reckon not." He snapped off the Geiger counter switch. The silence rode in upon them.

Milly looked about, restless in the shadowy cave. "I don't know what I expect from a man, but I do know I never find it."

"Don't you?"

"I know I'm looking for *something*. You know? And I keep feeling like I'll find it somewhere."

"What you figure you're looking for?"

"What?"

"What you reckon you got to have?"

"Well, I don't know.... I mean, if I was smart enough to think that out, I'd be all right, maybe. Maybe. I do know I've met plenty of guys that I thought could give me what I want — "

"Have you?"

"Well, sure. I mean, every girl wants *something*. And believe me, some of them want some pretty wild things. But not me. It seems kinda simple what I want, but just the same I never find it."

"Like what?"

She stirred, uncomfortable. "You keep trying to make me think."

"No, I don't. You said none of them had ever given you what you wanted. What did you want them to give you?"

"Well... that's it! Can't you understand what I mean? I don't know exactly. Maybe I'm crazy, maybe there isn't anything like what I'm looking for. All I know is that I've been looking for a long time, and every time with some new man, I think I've finally found it. But I never have. Like, well, take Reed. I was really crazy about him, all right. I married for love, I mean, really and truly... I thought sure Reed would give me what I wanted."

"But it didn't work out that way?"

She shrugged. "I don't have to lie to you. You can see for yourself where we are, Reed and I. I guess it was just sex with Reed and me. Animal. Huh?"

"Nothing wrong with animals. They get along one hell of a lot better than humans."

She frowned. "Well, maybe that's not what I mean. But, like, well, all Reed and I had was — going to bed and like that. He'd tell me how much he loved me, and wanted me, and sometimes it was real nice, but after a while — well, it wasn't what I wanted."

"So you decided to try Harve?"

"You make it sound pretty crude. I mean, it wasn't really like that. Reed gets all excited and all, worked up over what's happening — well, maybe he is really unhappy — "

"He looks pretty unhappy — "

"But it's all in his mind. Don't you think so? I mean, if he would just make up his mind that he and I are through — like finished — that he just hasn't got what I want — you see what I mean?"

"Sure. I see what you mean all right."

She stared at him. "You sound like you know what I mean, but you don't look like you like me very much."

He laughed. "Do I have to like everybody I understand?"

Her face paled, troubled. "Don't you like me, Josh?"

"What difference would it make?"

"Well, I like people to like me and all. I like people, and I like for them to like me. I get nervous — and drawn-up when people don't like me."

"I like you."

"Really? Do you think I'm pretty?"

He smiled. "I really do. I never saw anything like you since the dance hall closed here in Lust. And that was a long time ago. I was just a kid, but I used to press my face against the window, staring at them girls with long black stockings and short ruffled skirts, and the pink bare flesh between those skirts and what they wore at top. I used to ache, looking at them — "

"A little boy!" She was shocked.

"I was six, seven… but I wasn't small for my age."

"Goodness. You must have been a bad little boy."

"I would have been, if they had let me." He moved away from her and she followed, staying near the light, clinging to his shirt-tail. "But never mind me. We were talking about you.... What do you reckon Ole Harve can give you?"

She sighed. "Well, you make me sound so — sort of hard and mercenary — and I'm not, really. I'm real simple, and I try to be nice... I really do. You don't think I want to hurt Reed, do you?"

He shrugged.

"Well, I don't! I want him to go away and leave me alone. He can find some nice girl that will just love going to bed with him — he's — real good in bed, and he loves it — all the time. He used to come home, even to lunch, until I just had to tell him — "

"I see."

"Don't say it like that. A man like Reed. He can kill a girl. Especially me. All the men think I'm just crazy about sex, maybe because I'm pretty, and have a nice body, and they think all I care about is sexing. But that's not true. I want to have fun, and I want to be loved — oh, I mean in a different way — sometimes. It's hard to explain, but I sure didn't get that with Reed, I can tell you. He wanted to go to bed with me — anytime, anywhere."

"You had it tough."

"Maybe you think I didn't. But pretty soon, it looked like that was all he and I had together. And if any other man was nice to me, Reed got perfectly furious, and we'd fight — at least, he'd fight — and I'd get all drawn-up inside. You know? And dry. And he'd expect me to be able to love him just the same. And well, I just couldn't do it. I can't fight with a person one moment and then go to bed with him the next."

"So, you had nothing but fighting and fooling with Reed. What do you think about Harve?"

"Well, it's different with Harve. He wants to give me things. And well, it's pretty nice having a man giving you things instead of taking all the time. And poor Harve. He's worked so hard, and all he wants is to have fun — and take me with him. He's real proud of me, my looks and all, and he loves for people to look at me and admire me, even other men, and I can tell you this is pretty different from the way I been living with Reed."

He leaned against the stone wall. "You know what I think?"

"No. But I'd be awfully interested hearing. I never met any man like you before."

"You tell that to all men."

"Yes, but this time it's true. I tell people what I think they'll like to hear. But it's true now — whether you like it or not."

"Oh, I like it. I haven't liked anything so much since I used to smell the powder and perfume them dance girls used to wear. Got a sweet, creepy feeling at the nape of my neck — you ever have a sweet, aching feeling like that?"

"Not about women, silly."

He shrugged. "Well, just the same. Sometime you'll get that creepy, sweet aching feeling — like something you just can't stand, yet you know you'll die if it stops — then you'll know what you really been looking for all this time."

"Maybe. I been looking for a long time. I never found what I wanted."

"Know why? Because you're scared. And as long as you're scared, you never will find what you want."

She laughed. "Scared? Me? I never met a man that scared me."

"No. You're not scared of men. You're scared of yourself."

"That's silly. Why would I be scared of myself?"

"Because there's something wrong with you — "

"What's wrong with me?"

"Well, you're a liar, that's one thing that's wrong."

"I never lie. I tell the truth. Even when it's painful, still I tell the truth. You heard me talking to Reed... I didn't want to hurt Reed, but I had to tell him the truth."

"Sure. You tell the truth — to other people."

"What are you talking about?"

"You. You're lying to yourself. All the time. You keep looking for a man to give you something. Give you something. Give. What some man can give you. A lot of people are like that. That's why divorce lawyers get rich. Stop telling yourself you are looking for what somebody can give you. What do you offer a man, Milly? What do you give a man?"

"Why — I give him everything. Everything he wants."

"What do you give?"

"Oh, stop it. I don't know. Whatever they want — and it's usually the same thing."

"Is it? What about Harve? You're like a new car, a new suit, a new mansion to Harve — a new corporation he's taken over. That's what you give him. Because you're beautiful. And that's the truth about what you really want — men to see you're beautiful and give you everything."

"That's not true!"

"It's true, all right." He reached out, caught a handful of dust and spider webs and smeared it across her face.

Milly gasped and staggered away from him.

"I just messed up your pretty face, Milly. You look like hell. Like the wrath of God." He stalked after her and she backed slowly away, staggering on her high heels, eyes distended. "Suppose you were ugly, Milly? What would you give a man?"

Milly's back struck a wall. She looked about in panic. "Let me alone!"

"I'm not going to touch you, Milly. I don't want you."

"You're lying! You want me. I can see it in your face."

He moved closer. "You just see what you want to see, Milly. Everybody's got to give, and you take — and the hell with giving anything."

"That's not true."

"It's true, Milly. You're like those girls in the dance hall. They knew what they wanted — any man who had the most gold in his poke, and they got it."

"You're a liar." She grabbed his arms, digging her fingers into him, troubled. "You want me."

"I don't want you."

She thrust her mouth against his, moved her head, writhing her parted lips against his lips, thrusting her hot tongue into his mouth.

"You want me," she whispered, breathless. "You know damned well I can give you what nobody else can give you."

She kissed him again, pressing her body against him, teasing him, trying to torment him with all the tricks she'd ever learned or heard about, all the tricks that had had men crawling at her feet since she was twelve years old.

He held her away from him. "It's no good, Milly. You might as well stop."

She cried out, frightened. "What's the matter?"

"I've wanted plenty of women in my time. But I've learned something, Milly. You want a woman, that's fair enough. But — if she wants you — that's what God meant when He created heaven. When a woman stops thinking about what you can give her, and thinks about what she wants to do to keep you happy — "

"I don't know what you're talking about, but I do want you, Josh. I — wanted you when I first saw you."

"You want every new man, Milly. It's a game. It proves you're Milly Hall, still knocking them dead, taking home all the prizes."

Trembling, she moved against him. "No. It won't be like that...

I'm telling the truth. Maybe I have lied all my life, Josh, but I want to please you now, Josh... I'm not lying now, Josh ... you see if I am! You see if I am!"

24

"Oh God," Milly said, clinging to Carrdell. "What am I going to do?"

He yawned, holding her in his arms against the cave wall. "About what?"

"About you." She kissed along his cheek. She smiled, because the cave was warm now, no longer frightening and dark. Even the thick webs were a pleasant gray against the shadows.

"You don't have to do anything about me... not now."

"But I do." She breathed in deeply. "I know now what you were talking about... about wanting somebody — instead of wanting what somebody could give you." She dug her fingers into the thick muscles of his shoulders. "I don't know what I was when I came down here in this tunnel with you — maybe everything you said I was — but I'm not like that any more. I feel so strange, so good. Like I'm not even the same Milly Hall any more."

"One easy lesson," Carrdell said.

"One very easy lesson." She raked her parted lips along the line of his jaw. "You taste good."

"Lye soap," he said. He exhaled. "Too bad you couldn't stand this place."

"What do you mean? Your town? I love it. I love you and I love George. I love it all."

"No. It gets to be like a hell. Lonesome. You better check with my first wife about life in Lust. Her name was Fran. She couldn't stand this place. Got so she couldn't stand me. Everybody needs other people... and you — you need them a lot more than most."

"Maybe I don't — "

"Don't start lying to yourself again."

"I'm not, Josh. I could stay up here in this mountain — with you, I could. I'd never be scared. Or lonely. I only ran with crowds because — I didn't know what to do with myself.... You don't know what it's like. You're afraid to be alone because you can't stand yourself and your thoughts, you can't stand to be alone with what you know you are. I wouldn't feel that way with you."

He laughed. "It might last a week."

She stroked his face with the backs of her fingers. "If I had just a week of you — what we had — what we could have together — " She laughed in an excited, little-girl way. " — What I could do for you, the way I could love you. If I had a week of that, it might be better than a lifetime of what I've had." She pressed closer. "But it wouldn't end. Ever. I could tell. From the first minute. You'd always know how to treat me."

He laughed. "Sure. I'd bathe you in uranium every morning."

Laughing, she nuzzled against him. "But wouldn't that make me radioactive?"

"Honey, on you, nobody would ever notice it."

She scrubbed her head against the corded muscles of his chest.

Then she looked up, her face clouded, troubled. "Oh God, you are right. I am so terrible. Until now I never knew how bad. I ran away from Reed, and hurt him so. Now I've got to tell Harve I can't go to Mexico with him... no matter what... I couldn't possibly go to Mexico with him now. Oh, Josh, what's the matter with me? What am I?"

"Just like everybody, Milly. Just trying to find happiness on this earth. That's all."

"You make it sound so simple."

"Lord knows, it is simple. That's the whole answer. People trying to find a little happiness."

"I can't go around hurting people all my life."

His voice was level. "If you hurt Duncan now, you won't hurt him later."

She chewed at her lip. "That's true, isn't it?" She breathed out slowly. "Poor Harve. He's so nice. I hate to hurt him."

"You walked out on Reed — "

"That was different! I was different then — I just didn't know — "

"Still, you thought you were doing the best thing for Reed — "

"No. Not really. I knew it was best for me. I got to be honest."

"And now?"

She nodded. "You're right. I've got to tell Harve the truth. At least, this time, it really is best — for him." She pressed herself against Carrdell, but felt his body going tense, and he sat up, holding her away from him.

"What's the matter?"

He didn't have an opportunity to answer. Lantern light splashed across them. She slapped down at her dress and swung around on the lush padding of her hips.

Fletcher stood there, playing a brightly lit lantern into their faces. "All right, love birds. You've had your little fun. Let's go. I've fooled around with you long enough, Carrdell. One way or another, you're coming across with those distributor caps." His voice lashed at them. "Come on! On your feet."

Daybreak illumined every corner of the lobby with an egg-yolk yellow.

Carrdell and Milly came through the open trap door first, followed by Fletcher with pistol and lantern in his hand.

Fletcher slapped the trap door closed. All the people in the room were awake. Even Matt Bishop was reclining against the arm-rest of the couch. Susan sat beside him, poised, listening. Then they saw that the others were listening to something, too, from outside the hotel.

The front door was pushed open. A wan shaft of sunlight spilled thinly through it. Poole stood just inside the doorway, gun ready, turned so he could watch the people inside the room as well as the street.

Carrdell moved toward the couch, frowning, his head cocked as he listened. There was the distant whirring sound of an engine, growing slowly louder as it approached.

"Not a car," Carrdell said. "Engine runs too free."

Fletcher's lank face was gray. "I can tell you what it is, farmer. Helicopter. Damned state police whirlybird." He followed Carrdell, clipped him across the neck with the side of his gun so Carrdell spun around. "Time just ran out for you, tough boy. Where's those distributor caps? Even with that junker trailing us, the kid and me can make a run for it. Otherwise, I'm dead anyhow, and I'm putting a bullet in you."

Carrdell shrugged. "Go ahead. Kill me. You'll still be caught, you'll still rot in a jail."

"I ain't going back to prison. Stop stalling."

"I'm not stalling, Fletcher. You are. I gave you my deal. Named my price. All the dough. Turn it over to me, and — "

"For what?" Fletcher was trembling. Shadows swirled in his eyes, and every second it was more difficult to control his rage. "So I can make a run — broke — with the cops on my tail?"

"You'll still have a chance to make it. You said so."

"Broke." Fletcher stepped forward, raging but watchful.

Carrdell shrugged. "You can't have everything."

"Go ahead. Stall. If I don't get away, still I put bullets in you — for fun. You read me?"

Carrdell's voice was soft, even. "You don't have to be caught."

Fletcher got a fresh grip on himself. He listened a moment to the straining whine of the distant engine. He said, low, "I'm listening."

"Why, I can hide you. Poole. Bishop. Just like I hid the distributor caps. I can hide anything up here so nobody ever finds it."

"Go on."

"That's it. You two hide in the tunnel. When the helicopter is gone, you make a break for it."

"And the price?"

"The price is the same, Fletcher. Only your bargaining time is running out." He listened a moment to the motor. "Stop throwing away your only chance to stay alive. There are other banks, but you won't get a second chance at living."

You could almost see the wheels screaming around, grinding and screeching behind Fletcher's deep-set eyes. He was thinking about the helicopter, the money, the police coming in here, the chances of hiding, and then afterward, with Carrdell and that money, when the cops had pulled out.

He stared at Carrdell, then at Poole, at the other people, sweating. The sound of the helicopter was loud, climbing up the cliff to the ledge where Lust was. "My car's out there — plain sight."

"You got to trust me. I'll send them into the hills looking for you — in a different car — doesn't that make sense?"

"I hear you."

"They don't know how many cars were up here."

Fletcher sweated that one out. The helicopter was louder.

"You better trust me, Fletcher. I'm the only hope you got. But pretty soon now, it won't matter."

Fletcher hesitated less than a second now, but it was a long time; it was a slow eternity for him.

He strode out of the room, ran across the street to the roofless adobe. He came back in seconds, sweating, with the black suitcase. He took long strides across the room, listening to the helicopter grinding up the side of the mountain. He hurled the suitcase across the couch. Carrdell caught it easily.

There was no expression in his face, no triumph or surprise. This was the only ending the whole deal could have had.

"The copter!" Poole yelled, coming across the room from the opened door. "It's out there, Fletch. Over the side of the cliff."

Fletcher didn't look at him. He was staring at Carrdell's face. "Cross me, Carrdell. Cross me now and that money won't buy you anything but a grave."

Carrdell was already jerking open the trap door. "I got no reason to cross you." He flipped open the suitcase. He spoke to Matt. "This look like all the loot?"

"Hurry," Fletcher snarled.

But Carrdell waited until Bishop had nodded, keeping his face lowered.

Carrdell stepped aside, picked up the Indian rug. Poole and Fletcher went into the trap door. Carrdell and Susan helped Matt across to the opening. He went down slowly, breathing in a tired, anguished way.

The copter was violently loud, settling in the street outside the hotel.

The copter engine was cut off, and the silence gushed back thicker than ever. Carrdell closed the trap door easily and spread the scabrous old rug over it. He got up then and placed the black suitcase under the old hotel registration desk.

25

Nobody in the lobby moved, nobody spoke; they sat stiffly, like bad actors in a poorly directed play.

The front door was pushed all the way open, scraping dryly on the floor. Sheriff Ben Pritchard came through it, gun drawn. The only sound was a sigh of recognition from Harvey Duncan.

A stout deputy in khaki followed. His dark hair was churned as though it had been whipped by the propeller blades.

Carrdell leaned against the desk. "Howdy, Sheriff. Pete. Man, are we glad to see you."

Ben Pritchard paused just beyond the couch. His gaze grazed across the people before him. "Where are they?"

"Who?"

"Come on, Josh. Don't play games with me. I want those three men that held up the bank in Yucca City." Carrdell put on a mask of deep sincerity. "They were here all right, Ben."

"Where are they?"

"— more excitement than the old days when you and I were kids in this town, Ben —"

"Where are they, Carrdell?"

Carrdell glanced at the other people in the room. He said, with deep local pride in his voice, "Will you folks look at that Ben Pritchard? All business. He was born here in Lust. Same as me. But you wouldn't think it to look at him. I travel with donkeys and he rides copters. You sure come a long way, Ben —"

"You asking for trouble with me, Carrdell?"

"Why would I do that?"

"I trust you just as little as I do them three crooks I'm after."

"Ben, I wouldn't try to cross you —"

"You'd try to cross anybody —"

"No, sir. You're too smart for me, Ben."

"Just remember that, you damned, dry-land pirate. Where did those men get to?" He heeled about, facing the others in the lobby. "Who are you people?"

He recognized Milly and Harvey J. Duncan. "My God. You

two. I might have known."

"Hello, Sheriff," Milly said.

"Sheriff, I feel it my duty to tell you — " Harvey began.

"Wind comes right through these walls, they're so thin, is what Mr. Duncan is complaining about, Ben." Carrdell's voice was smooth, but he was warning Duncan.

Duncan realized in that instant that Carrdell was warning him that Fletcher, below this flooring, could hear him, and would kill him for betraying them to the police, even if he were caught. He would kill anyone who betrayed him. Fletcher was a terrible man for evening scores.

"Yeah, Duncan? What you got to say?" Ben Pritchard was a smart man, too. Nobody had to tell him that Carrdell had warned Duncan to keep his mouth shut.

"Just — that I wanted to tell you, those men were here, and unless you get them, we're all in danger."

"I already knew that," Ben said, staring at him.

But Duncan was a man who could bluff his way out of corners. "I felt it my duty to warn you, you'll need a bigger posse than you've got to arrest them."

Ben's mouth twisted, blue eyes chilled. "Don't try to tell me how to run my business, Duncan."

Carrdell smiled. "You see, Mr. Duncan? Cops never appreciate anything you try to tell them."

"Shut up, Carrdell," Ben said. "You want to talk, you tell me where those men got to."

"I want to," Carrdell said. "If you'll give me a chance. Like I told you, they were here. But you made one hell of a lot of noise coming up in that flying crate out there. They took off."

"I didn't see them."

"They didn't wait around to wave bye-bye, Ben," Carrdell said. "They heard you when you were miles away, down on that plain. They took off in my jeep for the hills. In a jeep they figure they can get lost among those boulders and shelves, and you'd never flush them out."

Ben shrugged his shirt up on his shoulders. "You think I won't? We got them pinned down. In this range. It's just a matter of time. And I'll tell you this, Carrdell. You think you know this country up here. I know it, too. Don't forget I was born up here, trailed around as much as you did. Only I had sense enough to get out of here — and stay out."

"Everybody always said you had a big head on your shoulders, Ben," Carrdell said.

"I hope you're smart enough to stay out of this, Carrdell," Ben told him. "Pete and I will sweep those uplands with the copter. But we'll be back. Don't you forget that, Carrdell."

Carrdell looked pained. "Why how could I forget it, Ben? Why, I'd expect you to come back."

Ben was already at the front door. "You better expect me, Josh. And God help you if you're lying to me again."

"Lying?" Carrdell looked wounded.

"Yes. Lying. You're the biggest liar that ever made twenty cents worth of uranium react like a bonanza on that Geiger counter you got there. You go ahead. You lie to everybody else. But don't try to lie to me."

He strode out. Pete followed him. Carrdell glanced at Milly. She was staring at him, at the Geiger counter on the desk top beside him, and back to him.

He tried to smile. "That Pritchard," he said, voice lame. "Always talking too much. Making trouble for everybody. It wasn't a big head folks used to say Ben Pritchard had — what they said was, he had a big mouth."

Nobody spoke. Carrdell looked at Milly a moment, then he shrugged. He walked across the lobby, stood in the front doorway, and watched the helicopter swing abruptly upward, taking off like a scalded hawk toward the timberline above them.

"That man is never going to forgive me," he said aloud.

Susan had pulled the trap door open.

"Matt," she called. "You all right?"

There was a moment of tense silence, and then Susan, searching the dark tunnel below her, screamed. She turned on her knees, crying. "Mr. Carrdell. It's Matt, Alone down there. He's fallen on the ground."

Carrdell crossed the lobby with long strides. He swung himself down into the tunnel without touching the steps. He lifted Matt in his arms, and climbed the ladder into the lobby. Carrying Matt across his shoulder, he went to the couch and laid him down on it.

Matt opened his eyes. They were glassy, slow to focus.

"Sorry... passed out. Standing there. Fletch decided to follow the tunnel. I — tried to go with them. But — couldn't make it."

Carrdell nodded. He turned, closed the trap door, tossed the rug over it.

Matt said, "Fletch is smart, Carrdell. You got to give him that. You got to watch him ... he means to kill you for that money."

Carrdell nodded. "Sure he does."

He knelt on his knee beside the couch as the front door was thrust open, and Fletcher burst through it, gun drawn. Poole was close behind him.

"Thanks, sucker," Fletcher said. His eyes ate into Carrdell like vile acid. "You pulled that hick sheriff off just long enough for Poole and me to make a run for it... now, give me that suitcase."

"They're looking for you in a jeep."

"Quit stalling. Looking for me and taking me is like two things," Fletcher said.

"We found your jeep," Poole said. "You didn't foul it."

Carrdell shrugged. "Always hated tearing up anything that belonged to me."

"You ain't worth a dime to me now, Carrdell. So this is like goodbye." The gun in Fletcher's hand came up.

Poole said, "Fletch. He's mine."

Fletcher snarled. "Take him then. I'm wasting no more time. Let's burn out of here."

Poole stepped around Fletcher. Carrdell threw himself low behind the couch, thrusting his hand beneath it. Fletcher yelled, jerking up his gun again.

He did not fire. George snarled and lunged at him. With a cold laugh, Fletcher turned deliberately from the couch and shot the big dog in the mouth. He fired twice and the mongrel staggered back, striking the floor heavily, already dead.

Duncan gasped, crying out in rage, "You rotten damned savage."

He moved without thinking, his hands out like claws, rushing at Fletcher. Wincing, Fletcher turned with gun ready, waiting for him.

But Duncan stopped in the middle of a step, as though a cosmic fist had struck him in the chest. He clutched both hands at his chest, digging at the fire there, the lancing pain, mouth wide as he gasped for breath. Frowning, Fletcher watched the big man double up, gasping, clutching at his chest, and fall to the floor.

Milly cried out and ran to Duncan. She sank to the floor beside him.

In that flash of time, Fletcher turned from them. But at that moment, Carrdell showed himself behind the couch with an old revolver in his hand. He did not even hesitate but fired point-blank at Fletcher.

Fletcher was struck, dead center, in the chest. The impact of the big forty-five sent him reeling backward, crazily, on his heels. He skidded and sprawled half through the door in the sunlight. He was dead and did not even writhe.

Poole hesitated a fraction of a second, staring at Fletcher, then whipped around bringing his gun up.

Reed was beside Poole, and he lunged, arms outward, as he hadn't tackled anybody since his Texas A.&M. days. He took Poole over hard on his side. The gun went off, but the bullet tore through the hotel roofing.

Carrdell sprang around the couch, moving lightly and swiftly on the balls of his feet. He kicked the gun out of Poole's fist, and in that second, all the fight went out of Tom Poole....

Reed released him, and stood up slowly, grinning to himself.

Carrdell turned and stared at the dead mongrel, and Poole lunged toward the gun.

He got his hands on it and swung around. Milly screamed.

Reed yelled a warning.

Carrdell, his face gray, swung around. He crouched and fired. Poole did not even press the trigger of his gun. He went toppling over on his back.

Carrdell stood there, arms slumped at his side. He let the gun fall from his fingers and stood looking at the dead men and the dead dog.

26

Milly got her arms around Harve Duncan and helped him to a straight chair. She was thinking that this might be a preview of the rest of her life. Ironic. Kind of what she deserved. She had wanted Harve so badly, well, she had him.

But Harve did not seem truly aware of her. He sat on the chair, thinking that from now on, as long as he lived, he would probably be depending on someone to help him to a chair. My God. Me. After the kind of life I've lived... Still, it was as if he were truly seeing himself as he was for the first time.

Reed looked at Poole, then at his hands, thinking it felt good tackling that killer, yanking him off his feet, the way he hadn't done since football games in another lifetime. It made you feel good, almost like a man. Almost as if you could be a man again, somehow. His gaze traveled to Milly and Duncan, stopped.

The sound of the returning helicopter was loud. Reed walked slowly to the opened door, watched the whirlybird hover, lower itself into the street.

Carrdell did not move.

He lifted his head only when Ben Pritchard strode back into the lobby, followed by his wind-churned deputy.

"All right, Carrdell," Ben said. "Smarted me again. Didn't you? Sent me scrambling out of here and — " He stared at the body sprawled in the doorway, and at Poole's body crumpled near the stairs. "What you trying to prove, Carrdell? Trying to go on making me look like a fool the rest of your life?"

Carrdell merely looked at him. His face was bleak. "You lied to me, Carrdell. Sure. I fell for it. I ought to have my head examined, falling for another of your lies." He raked his gaze across the dead gunmen. "But you nearly outsmarted yourself this time, didn't you?" Carrdell did not answer. He plodded slowly across the lobby, went behind the old desk, returned with the black suit-case.

Pritchard watched him warily, anticipating another trick. Carrdell thrust the suitcase on the kitchen table. Pritchard jerked his head, and Pete opened the black leather bag. He caught his breath at the sight of the greenbacks in thick, tight stacks.

Finally, Pritchard nodded. "Okay. I'll take all this evidence and the bodies with me." He turned, staring at Matt.

Bishop turned slowly and their gazes met.

"You'll have to come along, too, young fellow," said.

Susan touched Matt's arm, but didn't speak.

"Sorry, m'am," Ben said. "There's talk your husband was inside man on this robbery. He was in on it all the time."

Susan swallowed hard, did not say anything.

"You see, m'am, it began to add up. Way them two robbers walked in like the bank was cased and ordered Bishop around without even speaking to the others, except to line them against the wall. Somebody gave a shoeshine boy ten cents to put in the parking meter outside the Yucca City National Bank where the getaway car was parked at eight o'clock last Tuesday morning. Shoeshine boy swears the man was Matt Bishop. Now none of this is conclusive, but it's got the bank and the cops over there to thinking hard."

Susan whispered, "Oh, Matt."

"If there's any mistake, m'am," Ben said, "like if the boy put the dime in the wrong meter, why it'll all be cleared up."

Matt got slowly, unsteadily to his feet. "All right, Sheriff. I'll go with you." He glanced at Susan. "Please don't hate me."

She shook her head. "I don't hate you... not now... I never could really. Not — even when I tried."

Matt held her a moment in his arms, wavering. Pete came around the couch, gripped Matt's arm, steadying him, and they went slowly across the lobby. Pritchard closed the suitcase, locked it, glanced around, and then followed them out into the street.

In thirty minutes, the lobby was bare, and empty and still, warm and dry with old heat, old memories, old excitements that passed, so only the heat and the silence remained.

Carrdell had remained in the center of the lobby. He stared at the body of the dog on the floor where it had sprawled when Fletcher shot him.

Carrdell's face looked gray and tired.

Susan said, "I want to thank you, Josh, for all you did. There — are no words."

He looked at her, pulling his thoughts to her., "You'll be all right. It won't be easy. But all the money has been returned... you'll be all right."

She nodded. She pressed his hand. She glanced at the body of the dog. Her eyes brimmed with tears. "It's you I'm sorry for — it's as if we came in here — and killed or destroyed everything you had."

She waited. He did not speak. She moved to the doorway.

Duncan was standing now, gray, but steady on his feet. He picked up his suitcase. "Mrs. Bishop," he said, "would you wait a minute."

Susan paused in the doorway, nodded.

Duncan did not look at Milly. "The doctor tried to warn me. But looks like the best warning is the one that stops you cold — right in your tracks."

Milly said, "Harve —"

He looked at her then, his eyes gentle. "We had a wonderful time, Milly. I want you to know that. Me. An old guy wanting just one last fling out of life before it was too late. What I didn't know was, it was already too late for me."

He took a checkbook from his inside jacket pocket, scribbled a check, handed it to Milly.

She stared at it. "Oh, Harve. I can't take this ... you don't have to give me anything."

"I want to, Milly. And the Caddy. I'm leaving that with you. I'll ride down the hill with Mrs. Bishop to the nearest airport. I want you to have it, Milly... you look better in pink than I do."

She bit her lip, nodded, eyes brimmed with tears. "Please, Harve, take care."

He nodded, smiled. He walked out, following Susan Bishop into the sunlight. Nobody spoke, and after a moment Susan's car motor hummed to life, and then it went away down the trail.

Reed came across the room. "We can go back home now, Milly. I'll try to do better. I can't promise... I'm just what I am."

She shook her head. "Please, Reed, don't make me go."

"My God, Milly. Don't you think I got some sense now? I'm

not trying to make you do anything. You can come back home with me — if you want to."

"Oh, Reed, please don't. It's too late. Even if it never was your fault — it's too late now."

"Milly. What will you do?"

She shrugged. "I don't know. Drive till the pink Caddy falls apart, I guess. Drink and eat until this check is gone. Oh, Reed, I'm sorry. It was all my fault ... but it is too late."

Reed winced. He moved toward the front door, turned. "I won't ever be able to forget you, Milly."

"But — maybe — someday — you can forgive me."

Reed stared at her, troubled, worried now about her, but no longer grasping and clinging to her.... He turned and went through the door.

Milly stayed there a long time after Reed was gone. She heard his car start, but did not breathe until she could no longer hear it on the trail down the hill.

"Josh — "

He did not look at her. He walked slowly to where George lay, lifted the dog in his arms.

"Josh," she said.

He was moving toward the front door. He spoke over his shoulder, "Get smart," he said. "Go on. Get out of here."

He walked through the front doorway, carrying the dog in his arms. It was closer than he'd ever held George since he was a puppy.

When she was alone, Milly looked around the lobby. She stared at everything for a long time. She could hear Josh digging a grave in the hardpacked soil. She shivered suddenly, walked out the front door.

27

Josh Carrdell crossed the veranda and entered the front door of the hotel. He paused, scowling at the unaccustomed stillness. He looked down, realized he still carried the shovel. He hurled it from him across the room, heard it clatter against the wall, somehow pleased by the ringing noise it made.

He glanced through the window, then stood looking about at the big empty room with sunlight streaming through dust, glittering in it. Funny how much emptier a room looked with dust sifting slow and visible in the sun shafts.

He shivered slightly at the oppressive silence. He had to get out of here. It wasn't good up here now. It wouldn't be pleasant to die alone up here. Everybody needed somebody.

He lifted the door on its hinges, closed it. He crossed the lobby in the sudden fearsome silence. He replaced his gun beneath the couch where he kept it in case of prowlers. He looked around. No wonder Fran had hated this place. He might as well admit it, he'd driven his wife away. He'd had his prospecting, but all she had had was this silence. She couldn't stand it, and finally she couldn't stand him.

He looked around, spoke aloud. "I'm sorry, Fran. All these years I blamed you. I'm truly sorry."

His voice died away, and the silence rushed in around him again, with depth to it.

Good God, he'd start talking to himself.

His jaw hardened, a small muscle working in it. He had to be honest now. Hadn't he been talking to himself all these years? He'd lied, pretending he was talking to the burros, and to George. He was like that ancient prospector he remembered coming in to Lust to the general store, when there was a general store. Coming in talking to himself, only barely aware of people around him, even when they laughed at him, and the boys taunting him because he was an old man talking to himself.

He glared around the room. He wasn't an old man, yet, but he wasn't young any more, and he might as well face the truth: he had been talking to himself for a long time. If George hadn't been there to growl back at him, he would have talked to the lizards and the horned toads, and the gila monsters. Face it. Face the truth.

He moved about the room, a big man moving with the alertness a man learns in the desert and the hills, where the next step could mean death unless you were faster than death was. While he was facing the truth, he might as well face the truth about the blonde

Hall girl. How he had wanted her, from the first minute! What a liar he had been. She was every sweet-smelling, half-dressed, long-legged dance-hall girl he'd ever dreamed about, only she was one hell of a lot more, too. And he had been as wild as she had been down in that tunnel. Wilder.

"Thank God she's gone."

He was startled at the sound of his own voice. He had to stop this talking to himself. He had to clear out of this place, that's what he had to do.

He was proud of one thing: he had let her go. He could have been sobbing on that floor, the way Reed had been, and he would never forget her, and always wonder where she was and what she was doing. He could have begged her to stay, and maybe she would have stayed, and they would have lighted up the mountains, a fire they'd see in Lordsburg... for a while. My God, what did he have to offer a woman like her?

He leaned against the old desk, scrubbed the palms of his hands over his face, eyes dry and burning.

He heard something at the door. Every instinct warned him to turn, set himself. Death was as close as the next step; you hesitated and died.

He did not move.

After a moment he felt a creepy sick-sweetness at the nape of his neck, an aching across the bridge of his nose. "Josh."

He turned slowly.

"What about me?" Milly said.

He tried to smile. "What about you!" It wasn't a question.

"I been sitting out in the car. Waiting."

"I saw it out there."

"I thought you might come out. Thought you'd at least say goodbye.... After all, we were — pretty chose — in that tunnel."

"It — wasn't the first time you were ever close."

"Don't hurt me, Josh. Please."

He nodded. "So long, Milly."

She tilted her head. Tears brimmed her eyes. "I don't want to go, Josh. Unless you want me to."

He looked at his hands. "I want you to."

"I could give you so much, Josh."

"But I haven't anything to give you."

"Maybe I don't care."

"I better tell you. I want you — it'll be a different kind of lonely up here — now that you've been here. I wasn't ever lonely before. I never knew what it was really like."

"That's the nicest thing anybody ever said to me, Josh."

"But — I'm an awful liar. Like Ben Pritchard said. I'm forty-five, and I hate to think I'm a failure. So I lie — about things — even to myself."

Her voice was gentle. "Things — like uranium?"

He nodded. "A man who'll lie about uranium will lie about anything."

She breathed in deeply, looking about, frightened and appalled at the drabness around her.

He was watching her. "You see how it is. You're lucky, to be rid of me, so quick."

"Sure." She gestured helplessly toward him "Only — I better tell you — I never met anybody like you before — so maybe you are what I've been looking for all my life, without ever knowing it."

"I'm a liar, Milly, a forty-five-year-old failure, living like a damned hermit. I even made that Geiger counter lie to you."

"But — you made something else, Josh. Something more important, that wasn't a lie. That creepy sweet feeling along the nape of my neck. I never had that before."

"You'd get tired, Milly — "

"The ache across the bridge of my nose... it was like nobody ever touched me before. I need you, Josh. Please — let me stay."

He nodded and she smiled uncertainly, then ran to him. They met beside the couch. She caught his hand and drew him down upon it beside her.

"You weren't lying about that, were you, Josh? That sweet creepy feeling — that's not a lie, is it?"

"No... and it's working on me right now, something fierce."

She laughed, hurling herself suddenly against him. "You lie so much. I don't trust you. You got to prove it."

THE END

HARRY WHITTINGTON BIBLIOGRAPHY

Vengeance Valley (1946)
Her Sin (1946)
Slay Ride for a Lady (1950)
The Brass Monkey (1951)
Call Me Killer (1951)
Fires That Destroy (1951)
The Lady Was a Tramp (1951)
Satan's Widow (1951)
Forever Evil (1952)
Married to Murder (1951; reprinted 1959)
Murder is My Mistress (1951)
Drawn to Evil (1952)
Mourn the Hangman (1952)
Prime Sucker (1952)
Cracker Girl (1953)
So Dead My Love! (1953)
Vengeful Sinner (1953; reprinted as Nightclub Sinner, 1954; abridged as Die, Lover, 1960)
Saddle the Storm (1954)
Wild Oats (1954)
The Woman is Mine (1954)
You'll Die Next! (1954)
The Naked Jungle (1955)
One Got Away (1955)
Across That River (1956)
Desire in the Dust (1956)
Brute in Brass (1956; reprinted as Forgive Me, Killer, 1987)
The Humming Box (1956)
Saturday Night Town (1956)
Sinner's Club (1956; reprinted as Teenage Jungle, 1958)
A Woman on the Place (1956)
Man in the Shadow (1957) [screenplay novelization]
T'as des Visions! (1957, France)
One Deadly Dawn (1957)
Play for Keeps (1957)
Temptations of Valerie (1957) [screenplay novelization]
Trouble Rides Tall (1958)
Web of Murder (1958)
Backwoods Tramp (1959; reprinted as A Moment to Prey, 1987)
Halfway to Hell (1959)
Lust for Love (1959)
Strictly for the Boys (1959)
Strange Bargain (1959)
Strangers on Friday (1959)
A Ticket to Hell (1959)
Connolly's Woman (1960)
The Devil Wears Wings (1960)
Heat of Night (1960)
Hell Can Wait (1960)
A Night for Screaming (1960)
Nita's Place (1960)
Rebel Woman (1960)
Trouble Rides Tall (1960)
Vengeance is the Spur (1960)
Desert Stake-Out (1961)
God's Back Was Turned (1961)

Guerilla Girls (1961)
Journey Into Violence (1961)
The Searching Rider (1961)
A Trap for Sam Dodge (1961)
The Young Nurses (1961)
A Haven for the Damned (1962)
Hot as Fire Cold as Ice (1962)
69 Babylon Park (1962)
Wild Sky (1962)
Cora is a Nympho (1963)
Don't Speak to Strange Girls (1963)
Drygulch Town (1963)
Prairie Raiders (1963; reprinted as by Hondo Wells, 1977)
Cross the Red Creek (1964)
Fall of the Roman Empire (1964) [screenplay novelization]
High Fury (1964)
Hangrope Town (1964)
The Man from U.N.C.L.E #2: The Doomsday Affair (1965)
Valley of Savage Men (1965)
Wild Lonesome (1965)
Doomsday Mission (1967)
Bonanza: Treachery Trail (1968; pub in Germany as Ponderosa in Gefahr)
Burden's Mission (1968)
Charro! (1969)
Rampage (1978)
Sicilian Woman (1979)

As Ashley Carter

Master of Blackoaks (1976)
Sword of the Golden Stud (1977)
Panama (1978)
Secret of Blackoaks (1978)
Taproots of Falconhurst (1978)
Scandal of Falconhurst (1980)
Heritage of Blackoaks (1981)
Rogue of Falconhurst (1983)
Against All Gods (1983, UK)
A Darkling Moon (1985, UK)
Embrace the Wind (1985, UK; pub in the US as by Blaine Stevens)
A Farewell to Blackoaks (1986, UK)
Miz Lucretia of Falconhurst (1986)
Mandingo Mansa (1986, UK; pub in the US as Mandingo Master)
Strange Harvest (1986, UK)
Falconhurst Fugitive (1988)

As Curt Colman

Flesh Mother (1965)
Flamingo Terrace (1965)
Hell Bait (1966)
Sinsurance (1966)
The Taste of Desire (1966)
Sin Deep (1966)
Latent Lovers (1966)
Sinners After Six (1966)

Balcony of Shame (1967)
Mask of Lust (1967)
The Grim Peeper (1967)

As John Dexter:

Saddle Sinners (1964)
Lust Dupe (1964)
Pushover (1964)
Sin Psycho (1964)
Flesh Curse (1964)
Sharing Sharon (1965)
Shame Union (1965)
The Wedding Affair (1965)
Baptism in Shame (1965)
Sin Fishers (1966)
Passion Burned (1966)
Remembered Sin (1966)
The Sinning Room (1966)
Blood Lust Orgy (1966)
The Abortionists (1966)

As Tabor Evans

Longarm on the Humboldt (1981)
Longarm and the Golden Lady (1981)
Longarm and the Blue Norther (1981)
Longarm in Silver City (1982)
Longarm in Boulder Canyon (1982)
Longarm in the Big Thicket (1982)

As Whit Harrison

Body and Passion (1952)
Girl on Parole (1952; reprinted as Man Crazy, 1960)
Sailor's Weekend (1952)
Savage Love (1952; reprinted as by Harry Whittington as Native Girl, 1959)
Swamp Kill (1952)
Violent Night (1952)
Army Girl (1953)
Rapture Alley (1953)
Strip the Town Naked (1960)
Any Woman He Wanted (1961)
A Woman Possessed (1961)

As Kel Holland

Strange Young Wife (1963)
The Tempted (1964)

As Lance Horner

Golden Stud (1975)

As Harriet Kathryn Meyers

Small Town Nurse (1962)
Prodigal Nurse (1963)

As Blaine Stevens

The Outlanders (1979)
Embrace the Wind (1982)
Island of Kings (1989)

As Clay Stuart

His Brother's Wife (1964)

As Harry White

Shadow at Noon (1955; reprinted as by Hondo Wells, 1977)

As Hallam Whitney

Backwoods Hussy (1952; reprinted as Lisa, 1965)
Shack Road (1953)
Backwoods Shack (1954)
City Girl (1954)
Shanty Road (1954; reprinted as by Whit Harrison, 1956)
The Wild Seed (1956)

As Henry Whittier/ Henri Whittier

Nightmare Alibi (1972)
Another Man's Claim (1973)

As J. X. Williams

Lust Farm (1964)
Flesh Avenger (1964)
The Shame Hiders (1964)
Lust Buyer (1965)
Passion Flayed (1965)
Man Hater (1965)
Passion Hangover (1965)
Passion Cache (1966)
Baby Face (1966)
Flesh Snare (1966)

As Howard Winslow

The Mexican Connection (1972)

Harry Whittington was born in Ocala, Florida, in 1915. When his family moved to a nearby farm, Harry survived his family's rural poverty by reading books and sneaking into the local movie theater. Another escape was his writing. Ultimately the versatile Whittington would become known as "King of the Paperbacks," publishing over 170 original paperback novels, using nearly 20 different names. Before his death in 1989, Whittington also carved out a second career writing Southern historical novels as Ashley Carter. Today he is best known for the lurid and brisk noir novels he wrote between 1950 and 1960.

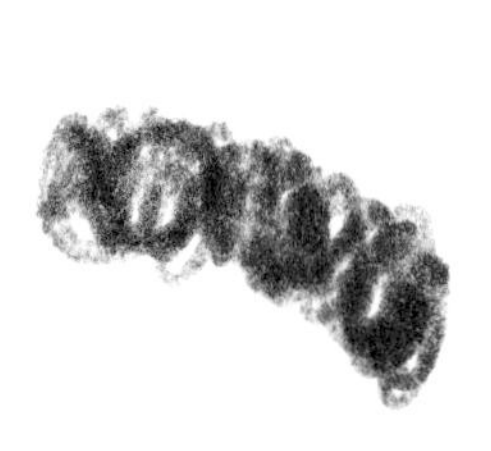

CPSIA information can be obtained
at www.ICGtesting.com
Printed in the USA
LVHW021639120619
621003LV00013B/441